MW00888314

The Lotus Enigma

A Novel

by

S.R. GIBSON

&

C. W. LUMPKIN

Published by Snowy Day Publications 2019

snowydaypublications@gmail.com

Hardy, Virginia 24101

Copyright 2019 Chuck Lumpkin

All Rights Reserved

All Characters are fictitious and any resemblance to anyone living or dead is purely coincidental. No part of this book may be distributed by any means without the consent of the authors.

ISBN 9781798501627

Edited by Jay Furick and Jack Brock

Foreword

The existence of teleportation has been argued for many years. Below are some accounts of the research we uncovered. This is not new. Many novels and movies have been made with the same assumptions. We believe that where there is smoke there is fire. We make no assertions of finding any factual accounts of the famous Philadelphia experiment.

The experiment was allegedly based on an aspect of some unified field theory, a term coined by **Albert Einstein** to describe a class of potential theories; such theories would aim to describe — mathematically and physically — the interrelated nature of the forces of electromagnetism and gravity, in other words, uniting their respective fields into a single field.

According to some accounts, unspecified "researchers" thought that some version of this field would enable using large electrical generators to bend light around an object via refraction, so that the object became completely invisible. The US Navy regarded this of military value and it sponsored the experiment.

There are no reliable, attributable accounts, but in most accounts of the supposed experiment, USS *Eldridge* was fitted with the required equipment at the Philadelphia Naval Shipyard. Testing began in the summer of 1943, and it was supposedly successful to a limited extent. One test resulted in *Eldridge* being rendered nearly invisible, with some witnesses reporting a "greenish fog" appearing in its place. Crew members complained of severe nausea afterwards. Also, reportedly, when the ship reappeared, some sailors were embedded in the metal structures of the ship, including one sailor who ended up on a deck level below that where he began and had his hand embedded in the steel hull of the ship, as well as some sailors who went "completely bananas."[15]

The conjecture then claims that the equipment was not properly re-calibrated, but that in spite of this, the experiment was repeated on October 28, 1943. This time, *Eldridge* not only became invisible, but she disappeared from the area in a flash of blue light and teleported to Norfolk, Virginia, over 200 miles (320 km) away. It is claimed that *Eldridge* sat for some time in view of men aboard the ship SS *Andrew Furuseth*, whereupon *Eldridge* vanished and then reappeared in Philadelphia at the site it had originally occupied. It was also said that the warship went approximately ten minutes back in time.

In 1955, astronomer and UFO buff Morris K. Jessup, the author of *The Case for the UFO*, about unidentified flying objects and the exotic means of_propulsion they might use, received two letters from a Carlos Miguel Allende[5] (who also identified himself as "Carl M. Allen" in another correspondence) who claimed to have witnessed a secret World War Two experiment at the Philadelphia Naval Shipyard. In this experiment, Allende claimed the destroyer escort USS *Eldridge* (DE-173) was rendered invisible, teleported to New York, teleported to another dimension where it encountered aliens, and teleported through time, resulting in the death of several sailors, some of whom were fused with the ship's hull.[6] Jessup dismissed Allende as a "crackpot".[6]

In early 1957, Jessup was contacted by the Office of Naval Research (ONR) in Washington, D.C., who had received a parcel containing a paperback copy of *The Case for the UFO* in a manila envelope marked "Happy Easter." The book had been extensively annotated in its margins, written with three different shades of pink ink, appearing to detail a correspondence among three individuals, only one of which is given a name: "Jemi." The ONR labeled the other two "Mr. A." and "Mr. B."

There may be classified evidence, that points to a team continuing the experiments in the US Air Force facilities at Area 51. The authors were not able to confirm this information.

Steve Gibson and Chuck Lumpkin

Chapter 1

Shanghai International airport

The fourteen hour flight from LAX to Shanghai arrived ten miuutes late. Dr. Wu Li Ming stood and stretched her sore muscles. She had a free ticket to Shanghai paid for by her under graduate school, Fudan University, to attend a physics symposium of international scientists sponsored by the Chinese government. The invitation email came only two days ago with no details. Her boss at Cal Tech did not hesitate giving her time off.

She was excited for the opportunity to visit her aunt, whom she had last seen almost a year ago. After her mom died, she had lived her teen years with her aunt in a tiny apartment over her aunt's bookshop.

Li Ming got up from her aisle seat and retrieved her backpack from the overhead bin, her only piece of luggage.

She got in the line of passengers standing to exit the plane. A few steps behind, a frumpily dressed woman carrying a small bag waited for an opening in the line.

The line moved slowly. The frumpy woman took her time. The line eventually came to the arrivals hall packed with people. A red dot suddenly appeared on the forehead of a woman next to Li Ming. Hair, skull and gray matter flew from the back of the passenger's head onto the following passengers. The only sound was like a melon being dropped. The woman toppled forward without a sound. Screams from the passengers behind Li Ming filled the room and people scattered. Li Ming ducked down instinctively.

No one seem to understand what had happened. Those passengers behind saw the woman's head explode and panic swept the room. Airport security officers were not sure what had happened and were yelling for everyone to remain where they were. No one paid much attention to their orders. The silent shot came from someone hidden. The people waiting for their passengers were separated from the arrivals hall by glass walls, so it meant the shooter was in the arrivals hall.

The security guards rushed to the fallen woman. It was apparent she had suffered a bullitt wound. The two security guards ran to the front of the hall. They pulled their weapons and were trying to determine where the shot originated.

Shots were fired. Screams came immediately. Li Ming felt a hand on her arm. The frumpily dressed woman whispered in Mandarin, "Do not look up, stay low and follow me." She crawled around passengers lying on the floor. Some were in shock; others were clutching their love ones. The woman, who appeared old, was very strong and pushed her way through the throng. When they reached the main hallway the woman pulled Li Ming to her feet and pointed at a door. More shots rang out accompanied by he sound of glass breaking. Li Ming turned to the woman. "Who are you?" She thought she may have seen her before, but was not sure where.

The woman looked directly into her eyes amd spoke in English, "No time to chat, walk at a normal pace and follow me before they shutdown the building." They walked through a door labeled No Admittance and down two flights of stairs. The woman pushed open the door at the bottom into a hall full of people totally unaware of what was happening above. The Customs and Immigration area was straight ahead. "Take out your passport and don't ask any questions. Get in the Chinese citizen line. I will be in the visitor's line."

Li Ming removed her passport from her backpack and held it tight in her shaking fist. Rows of officials were examining documents of arriving passengers. She could hear loud speakers giving directions to people she couldn't see. She dared not to look around and kept her head low as she waited behind the red line on the floor. She got a nod from an officer and placed her passport on the counter. The official looked at her, compared the picture and entered the passport number into his computer. He flipped through the pages and saw the USA Student Visa but gave it only a cursory glance then reached for his stamp machine and banged it down on an empty page and handed the passport back. She slung her backpack over her shoulder and headed to the Customs lines.

Li Ming saw the strange woman make a motion to follow her to a line at the customs check point. The line was moving along at a good pace. Several uniformed police were running towards an exit.

The woman, who did not look as old as Mi Ling first thought, put a small bag up on the belt moving luggage to the officials. She handed a declaration form to the officer and said in Mandarin, "Nothing to declare. I'm here on business." The Customs officer examined her passport and waved her through.

Li Ming put her backpack on the moving belt. When it reached the officer, she handed him her passport and declaration form. He looked at the form and opened the top of her backpack and looked at its contents. He handed the passport back and waved her through the check point.

An alarm went off and a flashing red light began to turn. The wobbling alarm was loud. Uniformed police were running down the hall. She slung her backpack over her shoulder and quickly headed toward the waving woman.

Li Ming thought the woman might be Asian, but was not sure. She was sure the woman spoke Mandarin with a Hong Kong accent. The woman waited at the exit which had a large sign in Chinese and English that read Ground Transportation. Without a word, the woman pushed open the door and they briskly walked to the rank of red taxis. It was a warm May Day, much like Pasadena in the spring but without the Shanghai smog.

Several people in uniform were yelling and running towards the exits to begin the process of locking down the terminal.

The woman opened the taxi door for Li Ming and spoke in Mandarin for the driver to take them to the Holiday Inn, Pudong. The driver nodded. The woman got into the taxi and they were off. Li Ming was shaken with all that had happened. The entire episode had taken less then five minutes. Questions in her mind came fast. *Who was this woman? Was the shooter after me? Why?*

"Who are you?" Li Ming realized she spoke in English. She had been in America for the better part of four years. She spoke English without thinking. The woman turned and spoke in hushed tones, "Not now, all will be explained later." She smiled at Li Ming and watched the driver look up in the rear view mirror. He most likely understood English. The woman took her cell phone out and tapped in a text message.

Half hour later

The taxi entered the south eastern suburbs of Shanghai and moved along at a good speed on the Inter Ring elevated Road. It slowed to make a right turn and entered a street with vendor's wooden carts cramed together. Li Ming saw a motorcycle come along beside the taxi and the rider point a large pistol at the taxi. Li Ming gasped, the only sound was glass breaking. The shards of glass flew into her face and hair as she ducked, the woman beside her didn't. The shot hit the woman in the right temple. Blood spattered on Li Ming's blouse. Another shot broke the glass in the front door. The taxi suddenly swerved and Li Ming was slamed into the back of the front seat behind the driver. She was dazed, shaking and confused.

The woman was thrown into the floor behind the front passenger's seat and slumped over against Li Ming. Li Ming couldn't get her breath. The woman was dead. She looked up and saw the taxi driver slumped over the steering wheeel. Li Ming's lower lip quivered and tears streamed down her face. It happened so fast. The taxi had careened over the curb and slammed into a bunch of vendor carts and stopped against a building. People were screaming and helping people to their feet. Pieces of vendor carts covered the car. Feathers flew into the air and vegetables streamed down the windshield.

The driver appeared to be dead. She grabbed her backpack and pushed against the door wth her right shoulder. It was stuck. She saw people looking at her. She gave a lurch into the door. There were heaps of debris from the vendor carts against the door. She shoved again with all her might. It moved and she finally managed to squeeze through the small opening.

A crowd gathered and began pulling debris away from the taxi. The motorcycle had stopped and the driver watched Li Ming struggle out of the wreckage. She saw the motorcycle driver but not his face which was hidden by a dark red helmet with a distinctive bright yellow lightning bolt. The machine sped away as soon as Li Ming stared at it.

The crowd pulled the broken carts away from the taxi and stared at the dead woman and driver. Li Ming blended into the crowd. Her right shoulder was hurting. She thought it was sprained or badly brused. She didn't know what to do, but had to get control of herself. Her whole body shook as she moved further away from the wreckage.

The street began to fill with people. In a daze she walked slowely along the street as curious people rushed past her to get a view of the crash.

Police sirens were getting louder. She was trying to think of what to do. *Do I dare go to the police? Why are people trying to kill me? Who was that woman?*

Li Ming walked many blocks without any destination in mind. She saw an intersection ahead and read the street sign, it was Zhulin Road. She knew she was not far from her aunt's bookshop. She stopped and opened her backpack and took out her iPhone. She entered in the number for her aunt's book store. She needed to make a plan and go someplace safe. Her aunt was expecting her but she did not want to put her aunt in danger.

When a man answered, Li Ming took a quick breath and her heart beat jumped to what she thought was a drum pounding in her chest. She knew a man should not be answering her aunt's phone. She ended the call and stood motionless. as a police car sped by. She had to get as far away from this area as possible.

She walked for many blocks and had no idea where she was, but the area seemed more familiar. She stopped walking. Her shoulder was hurting and her legs felt as if they would colapse at any moment. She took stock of her situation. *People are after me. Three people have been murdered. My aunt may be in danger. Why did a man answer my aunt's phone?*

She knew if she used her iPhone to call the police, they could trace her. She needed another phone. She saw a phone box across the street, but did not have any Chinese coins, she had forgotten to exchange US for Chinese money and did not want to go into a shop and try to exchange US dollars. She would be remembered for sure. There was no bank in sight. She saw the next intersection and decided to go see if a bank may be on the side streets.

She looked up and down the side streets but there were no banks. She spotted a young man speaking into a cell phone. She saw him end a call and place it in his jean's pocket. She had an Idea. She walked up to him, "I'll give five dollars US for the use of your phone." She pulled her purse from her backpack and removed a five dollar note. She handed it to the young man. "What is your name?"

"I am Xia Wang. He smiled and pulled the phone from his pocket and handed it to her.

She took the phone and walked a few paces away and tapped in 110, the emergency number. A woman answered, "What is your emergency?"

"I think there is a robbery in progress at Wu's Book Store." She gave the address. "Please hurry." She pressed the end key and handed the phone back to the young man. "If you get a call from the police, only tell them you helped someone in distress but nothing more." He looked at her and nodded. She smiled and turned to walk away.

The young man tagged along. "Where is the bookshop that's being robbed?" Li Ming stopped walking and told him the address. "That's not far from here. You can walk it in a few minutes."

Li Ming stared at the young man. "Thanks. Which direction, I'm sort of turned around."

The young man pointed. "You walk four blocks in that direction, then turn right for six blocks and you will find the shop." He looked at Li Ming's blouse. "Did you cut yourself; there is blood on your blouse."

Li Ming reached into her backpack for her compact mirror and observed the stain. "Oh, that is not blood, its tomato stain from my lunch." She smiled at the young man. He looked relieved. *If the police question him he will be sure to mention the stain, even if I lied that it was tomato juice.*

"If I may ask, will you walk with me? I might get lost." He looked hesitant but smiled.

They walked several blocks without any conversation. Li Ming asked, "How far are we from Fudan University?"

"Not far, you can ride the subway from Yangshupu Road and transfer to Danyang Road subway. It will take about forty-five minutes." He looked at her for some response.

"I went to that university. I haven't been back here for a very long time." Xia's eye brows went up.

"Wow it is the top university in China. My sister is going there now. She is in her last year."

"That's great. What is her major study?"

"She is taking Theoretical Physics", said Xia.

Li Ming stopped walking. She was thinking. "Xia, do you think you can contact your sister and let me speak to her?"

"Sure." Xia took out his phone and called his sister. "Zhon, this is Xia, I have a person here that graduated from your university and she would like to speak to you." Xia listened for a few seconds and then handed the phone to Li Ming. "Her name is Zhon Ping."

"Hello, my name is Wu Li Ming. I graduated several years ago and got a degree in Theoretical Physics. Xia says you are also in the physics department. Are you aware of some sort of symposium that is to take place?" Li Ming listened for a full minute. "Do you know who will attend?"

Li Ming reached into her backpack and took out her note pad. She jotted down several names. "Thank you so much. May I call you again?" She wrote down the number. "Zhon, don't tell anyone you spoke to me. I want to surprise them." She handed the phone back to Xia who listened for a few seconds and said good bye and ended the call.

They walked in silence for a block. "I heard you tell my sister that you are Wu Li Ming. She told me you are famous at the university." The sound of a siren was close.

"Yes my name is Li Ming and I'm afraid being famous is an overstatement."

They turned at the corner and could see blue flashing lights from several police cars in the distance. Li Ming drew a deep breath and her stomach lurched. She hoped her Aunt was not harmed. Xia looked at her drawn face and reached for her hand. She took it and picked up the pace toward the bookshop.

A small crowd had gathered in front of the shop. She thought it best to stay in the background until more was known. They walked to the back of the crowd. Several were speculating on what was happening. One woman said she had heard there was a robbery but was not sure. Li Ming nudged Xia and motioned for him to follow her into an alley across from the bookshop.

Two policemen came out of the shop and motioned for the crowd to disperse. People began to move away. As soon as most of the people were gone, three policemen came out with two men in handcuffs, they put them into a patrol car and whisked away.

Li Ming stepped from the alley and walked up to one of the officers. "Is the woman who runs the shop alright?" She looked carefully at the officer's face.

"Yes, she was tied up and scared but was not harmed." Li Ming let out a sigh of relief. She turned and walked toward the alley where Xia was waiting. She would not approach the bookshop today but would call her aunt later and explain she had a change of plans and would visit later in the week.

When she stepped into the alley, she heard the sound of a motorcycle approaching. She turned and saw the dark red helmet with the bright yellow lightning bolt. It was the same person that fired on the taxi. The bike passed by slowly as the driver stared at the bookshop with two policemen standing out front. Li Ming smiled. *Your buddies cannot help you now. Who are these people and why are they trying to kill me?*

Chapter 2

One Month Ago

Pyongyang, North Korea

Seok Dong-Suk, North Korea's master spy of the secret RGB, knew the North Korean military command was in disarray.

The North Korean leader had told his top military men the only war that mattered was a military one not an economic one. The commanders were given two years to be the superior force on the planet. They were far from achieving the goal. The military accidently discovered a secret experiment on a device that would propel their struggling army into a superior position.

Seok knew the importance of determining if the device actually worked. The information about the device was suspect. His agents reported their informant inside Cal Tech told them that a major discovery had been made by a Chinese exchange student named Wu Li Ming. She was a top Theoretical Physics student who had just received her doctor's degree and worked with Area 51 scientist.The discovery was history making.

There had been rumors for years a device being tested at Area 51 would change the world, according to a leading North Korean scientist.

Seok interviewed the North Korean scientist, whose father worked for the US Navy in 1943 and had witnessed an experiment that if true, would shake the foundation of modern physics. The father was not a scientist and did not know the nature of the experiment but his description of what he witnessed was unmistakable to his son. The scientist told Seok the device being tested was very theoretical but if it worked and he could get his hands on it, Korea's position in the world would change big time.

***

Their asset at Cal Tech confirmed there was a top secret project underway and was part of the experiments carried out at Area 51 but she did not know any details. Many scientists had been moved from Area 51 to Cal Tech. That in itself was very interesting. There had to be a reason to warrant such a move of classified research personnel.

She reported that security around the lab had increased over the past several months. Uniformed troops were now present in the halls and around the lab building. It would make surveillance difficult but they had to know if the device worked. North Korea's future depended on the possibilities of using the device.

Seok ordered his team to steal the device and all information concerning the device and leave no evidence of their presence.

***

At 4 AM, four men wearing ski masks entered the mechanical room below the lab building. There were no cameras in this area. The control box for the interior surveillance cameras was on the wall opposite the entrance. One of the men opened the control box and attached a device that played a loop video. The men monitoring the cameras in Cal Tech's security office would see only a repeating scene. The team had practiced the mission several times, and now it was for real. They wore gloves and had on booties over their shoes. One of the men opened the door to the main hall just wide enough to view two soldiers on guard. The man aimed his silenced weapon and pulled the trigger twice. The two guards slumped to the floor without a sound. The drug was instant. They were not dead.

The team rushed into the hall and removed the weapons from the fallen soldiers along with the keycards around their necks. The leader ran to the lab door and used the keycard to open the door. The team entered the lab and began to assess the equipment and computers.

"Grab that large device with all the wires and those two computers and the log book", said the leader. They disconnected the device and placed it into a large wooden box that was obviously made for the device. The computers were laptops and were easily carried by one man. Two of the men carried the wooden box. The leader grabbed a loose leaf notebook that was open on the lab bench.

The leader returned the soldiers' weapons and keycards. They entered the mechanical room and exited the building without an incident. The entire mission took less than nine minutes.

Their van sped through the suburbs of Pasadena. A truck waited for them to transfer the stolen items disguised as diplomatic cargo to be moved to LAX for shipment to North Korea. All went without a hitch.

Beijing, China

A quickly organized meeting took place in the Ministry of State Security (MSS). An agent in California reported that known RGB agents had been spotted near the Cal Tech campus.

Jai Chun, the master spy for China, was concerned. North Korea had been acting strange for the past year. Many millions of Yuan had been poured into supporting their neighbor. The Western Nations had put pressure on Beijing to stop their rambunctious neighbor's missile testing. China cut support and trade substantially with North Korea. It seemed to have worked. No missiles had been launched in months.

Jai Chun stared at the assembled group. They were all surprised the RGB had some of their best agents in a college town. "Gentlemen, this is a serious situation. We do not have any information as to what they are doing and why they are targeting the campus of Cal Tech. I want a report within forty eight hours giving me all the details." He gathered up his papers and left the room. There was not a word among the group. They each exited the room in silence.

The Chinese had many agents in foreign countries, mostly to steal industrial information. The MSS monitored most western nation's military activities and most of the larger spy organizations knew each of their rival players by sight. They were very careful not to disturb the status quo.

In an office down the hall from the conference room, Jai Chun sat at his large desk and composed a report to the President. He was careful not to make any predictions. He simply stated the facts. The President was a man that took all reports on face value. Each day, Jai had to brief the President on all the major activities monitored by the MSS. North Korea had been moved up the list of importance.

Jai Chun finished his briefing report, sat back and smoked his first cigarette of the day. He took the American's Surgeon General's warning seriously and limited himself to three a day. His phone buzzed. The caller ID indicated it was from one of his top department heads.

"Hello Wong, what can I do for you today?"

"Minister, we have an urgent report from our lead agent in Pasadena, California. May I have an appointment to brief you?"

"Yes, yes, come now." Jai Chun was surprised that his agents had gotten a report from the USA so quickly. He looked at the computer screen and deleted the part of the report concerning the Koreans. He would wait to hear the news before completing the report.

His secretary buzzed and informed him a department head was waiting to see him. He told her to send him in.

"Sir, we have received a report that several RGB agents entered one of the top secret labs at Cal Tech. Our informant said they made off with a large box and two computers. We do not have any more information at this time. I thought you might want to know that the North Koreans have stepped up their activity for unknown reasons. We will send agents to report exactly what is happening. I will keep you fully informed."

"Thank you Wong. Yes, I want to be kept up-to-date on all moves by the Koreans. Please phone me immediately upon receiving any reports. I want to know what was being worked on in that lab." The department head quickly left the office. Jai Chun printed his report for the President. He omitted any mention of the North Koreans until he had more information.

Lab 204 Cal Tech

The security people were everywhere photographing and looking for clues, while an Army Major was shouting orders. Sergeants were shouting. Li Ming stood off to the side. She knew that the device had been taken by someone. She thought it was a prank the students had come up with. She was relieved when a key component sitting in plain sight had been over looked.

Her note book had been taken but it was only notes relating to the power supply. The two laptops were another matter. They contained the main design and experiment results. The key component had not been added to the design as of yesterday's experiment. She could re-build the main device in a few weeks. An army officer asked her a few questions but was satisfied she had nothing to do with the theft.

Two civilians entered the lab, a man and a woman. The woman looked Asian. They identified themselves to Li Ming as agents from the FBI. They asked about what was missing and what was it used for. Li Ming explained that she was under instructions to refer any ques-tions about the function of the lab and its experiments to Dr. March, the head of the lab. The man did not like that answer. "Dr. Wu, we are here to help. We need to know what was going on in this lab." Li Ming smiled and again referred all questions about the lab to Dr. March.

"And where is Dr. March?" asked the woman.

"He will be here shortly. He is in the Chancellors' office at the mo-ment." With that the two FBI agents shrugged and walked over to the Major. Li Ming watched as they attempted to get information from the Major. They did not seem too successful.

Li Ming reognized the Cal Tech chief of security approaching. "Dr. Wu, you should be very careful to whom you speak. Even the government agents are not to be trusted with information about your experiments. Dr. March is on his way here. I suggest you go to your office and determine if anything is missing." Li Ming bowed slightly and walked to her office across the hall.

***

Her office was neat and the secret safe built into the wall had not been opened. The seal was still in place behind a picture of Ron-ald Reagan. Li Ming kept all of her personal notes and test results in that safe. Nothing of the experiments was kept in her desk. She sat and thought about the theft. No one would be able to make the device work without her special component and her detailed notes. Most would not understand the connection to the special device. Any

Theoretical scientist would know that the device was missing an important. component. If someone was intent on stealing the device they would be very disappointed in the result of any experiment. She was only days away from proving the device's function to Dr. March and his team from Area 51.

Chapter 3

Shanghai

Li Ming stood very still watching the motorcycle disappear from sight. She saw Xia watching her intently. She smiled and patted him on the shoulder. "Xia, I was going to stay with my aunt but I don't think it's a good idea to go there until I've had a chance to speak with her. Are there any small hotels in this area? I can't remember."

Xia backed away a few feet. "How did you know a robbery was taking place?"

Li Ming hesitated. "That's a good question. I suspected something may be going on when I phoned my aunt earlier. I just wanted to make her safe. If there had been no robbery, there would have been no harm." She hoped that little lie would help keep more questions at bay.

Xia thought for a moment or so. "I don't know of any hotels in the area. You can stay with my family. Zhon stays at the University so her room is available." Li Ming stared at Xia for a moment.

"That is very kind of you, but what will your parents say about you bringing a total stranger home to spend the night?"

"Hang on, maybe there is another way." He pulled out his phone and called his sister. "Zhon is there a way Li Ming can spend the night at the dorms. Her plans have changed and the place she was to stay will not be available until tomorrow." He listened for a few seconds. "Yes she is here, hold on." He handed the phone to Li Ming.

"Hello Zhon, I know this is very unusual but if there is a way you can accommodate me for tonight?" She listened for several seconds. "That's great. I'll be there in an hour. Thank you so much. Xia will be with me so you will know who I am." She paused. "I see. Was it distributed widely?" She listened. "Okay, I will meet you in an hour." She handed the phone back to Xia.

"Yes sister. I will show her the way. We will take the subway." He disconnected the call. "Let's go, it's several blocks to the subway station."

Xia knew the area well. They took shortcuts through alleys and courtyards. Soon the subway station was in sight. There was a bank on the corner next to the station. "Xia, I must stop at the bank to exchange some money." He nodded. She entered the bank and exchanged fifty dollars US for Chinese currency. Xia waited patiently outside. She returned in less than five minutes. "Okay, now I can pay for things without making a scene."

They entered the subway station. It had been years since Li Ming had ridden the Shanghai subway. They had made many changes. There was no ticket window; all tickets were issued from machines. She put the required amount for two tickets and was rewarded with the tickets spitting out of a slot. Xia laughed at her when the tickets popping out out startled her. "Well, I was not expecting the machine to make so much noise." She giggled. It was the first time in hours she felt normal.

The subway ride to the transfer station was fast. They waited ten minutes for the next train. It swooshed into the station. Even though the train was packed, they pushed their way onto the first car. The lurch of the train made both nearly fall before grabbing an overhead handle. Most of the passengers were middle aged. Li Ming thought they were workers either getting off shift or going on shift. The train pulled into the University Station.

The walk to the residence hall was short. Li Ming knew where the hall were located but during her time here she never stayed in the dorms, but only visited friends to study. She had always stayed at her aunt's small apartment above the book store and had taken the bus in those days.

She saw a tall girl in a Fudan sweat shirt standing outside one the entrances. Xia waved and the girl waved back. Xia introduced the two girls. Zhon was very pretty and dressed very well for a student. Li Ming was beginning to think that their family must be well off.

"Zhon it is very kind for you to accommodate me with such short notice."

"Li Ming it is such an honor to meet you. You are famous. You are the only student ever to score perfect for four years. Your picture is on display in the administration building and in the physics department. I knew it was you." Li Ming was slightly embarrassed by such admiration.

Zhon continued speaking, "My roommate is away this week. Come let me show you our room." Zhon led them through the entrance and up two flights of stairs. The room was halfway down the wide hall-way. There were no hall monitors. Li Ming remembered some of her friends complaining about the strict rules the dorm monitors imposed on all the students. Something had changed.

"Zhon there are no monitors. When did this change?"

"About two years ago. The administration suddenly changed and many of the old rules changed too. The new administration is very liberal. The students have much more influence in decisions." She opened the door to her room. It was not what Li Ming expected. The room was actually a suite of rooms. There were two bedrooms with a desk in each, with a private bath for each bedroom, and a sitting room with a large flat screen TV.

"Wow, I never knew the dorms were so nice. During my day, the dorms were made up of single rooms and a public bath on each floor. Times have changed."

Xia reached for the remote control to the TV. As it came on and a news bulletin was playing. The reporter was at the scene of a taxi crash earlier in the day. "Two people died here, but not from the accident. They had been shot. Police are looking for a female passenger who bystanders said left the scene. If you know any details that will aid the police call 110." The reporter went on to another story.

Xia and Zhon turned and looked at Li Ming. "Are you the one that left the scene of the accident", asked Xia.

"Yes. Twice today someone has tried to kill me. I don't know why or who they are. When I arrived at the airport, I was shot at and on the way to a hotel a man on a motorcycle shot at me in the taxi. At least three people have died because of me. My aunt was held captive by two men who thought I would go to the book store. There was silence. Zhon and Li Ming nodded at each other.

"Zhon, show me the flyer that is being circulated about the physics symposium." Zhon went to a desk in her bedroom and brought out a small flyer. The flyer had no pictures of the participants but only their names. Li Ming was listed as one of the scientists attending. The flyer said the symposium was about advanced Quantum Physics. Top level scientists from all across the world will be attending. The symposium is to be Friday at Fudan University Physics Department, but is not open to the public.

"Zhon, what was the purpose of the flyer if it is not open to the public." Li Ming stared at the flyer.

"I don't know. I got one in my box yesterday. I assumed it was from the Physics Department. Maybe they were proud to be hosting such an important group of scientists."

"Hum, maybe so." Li Ming was not happy about all that was happening. She decided to phone her aunt. *The police should be gone by now.*

The phone rang twice before Li Ming heard her aunt's voice. "Aunt, I am so glad to speak to you. I'm in Shanghai."

"Li Ming, so much has happened today. Will you be here for the evening meal? I have so much to tell you." Li Ming had called her aunt three days ago from Pasadena as soon as she knew about the symposium and that she was coming to Shanghai.

"No aunt. I am staying with friends this evening. It is so good to hear your voice. I too have much to tell you." She decided not to mention that she had seen the two men leave the shop in handcuffs and all the other events that had happened. "I will call you tomorrow afternoon. I'm attending the symposium in the morning. Until then, goodbye." She punched off the phone before her aunt could object to her not coming tonight. She felt guilty about what was happening, especially involving her aunt.

Li Ming sat down and relived all the events over the past 30 days. The bazaar events started with the theft at the lab, the sudden fully paid invitation to the symposium, the episode at the Shanghai airport, the taxi event, and her aunt's ordeal. Someone or group was after the technology she had been working on for the past four years. They must be desperate to take lives for their cause. Why would killing her make a difference? Then it hit her, they were trying to intimidate her but not kill her—but for what purpose?

She sat with her head in her hands. Xia and Zhon left her in peace. Something was bothering her. She tried to bring it to the surface, but nothing came to her. She decided to go back to the incident at the airport and replay in her mind all she could remember.

The frumpily dressed Asian woman who had helped her escape the airport kept coming up. She had seen her before but where. She was unremarkable in appearance. Spoke Mandarin with a Hong Kong accent. English was perfect American style.

Maybe if she went back to the theft. The device was stolen but not the special component. Most of the design was on the two laptops but missing the last experiment with the component. She thought about the army personnel who took control of the lab and the two FBI agents. BINGO, the frumpy woman was the female FBI agent. She had been followed from LAX by the FBI. The woman gave her own life to protect hers. The whole thing was absurd. Evidently the FBI feared for her safety. Why?

Chapter 4

Fudan University

Li Ming didn't sleep well. She kept waking and seeing the taxi crash. She was very tired. Zhon brought her a cup of tea and some food. She nibbled at the food and drank the hot tea. The symposium was in an hour. She took a hot shower and dressed in her only change of clothes from her back pack. At least she didn't have to keep the blood stained blouse on another day.

She placed her soiled clothes in a plastic bag and put them in her backpack. She removed her laptop and folder with all her notes. Zhon said she could leave her backpack in her room. The walk to the physics building was short. Zhon walked with her and explained all the new construction going on. It seemed to Li Ming the campus was full of new buildings. Construction cranes must be their new national bird.

They reached the physics building where several campus security guards were at the entrance. They explained the building was closed today for a special meeting. Zhon nodded and said bye to Li Ming and said she would see her back in her room later in the day. Li Ming opened her folder and removed the invitation. The guard examined the invitation and stepped aside to allow her entrance to the building.

The symposium was held in a large conference room across from the main physics lab. Li Ming entered the room to find several people she recognized from international publications. She was impressed. Each of the participants had name cards placed at their seats. She found her position and placed her laptop and folder on the table. As she took her seat, she noticed the North Koreans had a representative at the far end of the table.

The chairman of the physics department entered the room. He immediately recognized Li Ming seated to his right. He nodded. The gavel hit the block and he announced the symposium open. Several wore headsets to have the remarks translated from Mandarin.

Two assistants came in and distributed agendas and other information. Li Ming read the agenda and noted that nothing was on the agenda about her field of work. She wondered why she was invited. The last item on the agenda was to allow the participants to offer subjects for discussion. That would be interesting. She was curious as to what the other scientists were working on.

The symposium moved along from item to item on the agenda finally to the last item just before noon. The North Korean representative raised his hand. He was recognized by the chairman. "I have heard rumors that certain progress is being made in the Quantum field of teleportation. I know that one of our esteemed members has been involved in experimenting in this field for several years. I would like for her to tell us of her progress.

Li Ming was stunned with the question. She didn't know what to say. How did the Korean know of her work? It was top secret as far as she knew. She could not comment on her experiments without violating her oath and trust to Cal Tech. "My apology, I am not prepared to speak. In due time, I will publish any results that are positive regarding my experiments."

The Korean would not let it go. "My sources tell me you have been successful in your quest to prove teleportation is possible. Why can you not share with this group?" He stared at Li Ming.

"My esteemed colleague, when I am ready to release my findings, you will be one of the first I will send my published report to." She saw several heads nod in her favor. The American representative's name card said he was from MIT. He sat and smiled. He was handsome but his beard kept her from seeing his face.

The chairman banged the gavel. "I think we will move on to anyone else that has a topic for discussion." He looked around the room. One hand went up. The representative from Russia had his hand up. The chairman nodded at the Russian.

"Mr. Chairman, I too am curious about these rumors of Quantum teleportation. I would encourage Dr. Wu to share where she is in proving the theory." He smiled at Li Ming. The chairman looked at Li Ming for a response.

"Mr. Chairman, distinguished colleagues, as I said in response to the North Korean representative, I will publish my results soon. I am not prepared nor do I want to speculate on the outcome of experiments in my lab. I am sure several of you have heard of these rumors. I suggest you concern your thoughts with more practical matters, like global warming." The North Korean pulled a frown on his face and slammed shut his note book. The Russian smiled.

The chairman announced the meeting adjourned for lunch. He announced that the afternoon session was a hands-on lab experiment concerning light emitting diodes. The room filled with chatter as the participants slid back their chairs and began exiting the room. Li Ming noticed the Korean staring at her. His face said it all. He was pissed at something.

Li Ming did not want to attend the afternoon session. She approached the chairman and notified him of her decision to skip the remainder of the symposium. She turned to leave and saw two men approach the North Korean. They whispered something to each other. One of the men turned to stare at Li Ming. His stare was unnerving to her. She picked up her laptop and folder and started making her way to the door. She heard a voice whisper in English, "Don't turn around. Walk to the entrance door and exit to the court yard." She was startled but did as asked.

In the hallway, she turned toward the exit. She sensed more than observed someone close behind her. She pushed open the exit door and walked out on the vast steps leading down to the court yard. The presence was still behind her. She reached the court yard and turned. The American with the beard walked past her without turning. He spoke as he passed. "Follow me. You are in danger." She looked carefully at the man. She knew who he was, the FBI agent that had questioned her at Cal Tech during the robbery. What was going on? She turned in time to see the two Korean men looking around the court yard. They saw her and began to come down the steps.

She saw the American approach a black SUV parked at the curb. He opened the back door and held it for her.

He motioned for her to get into the car and got in beside her shutting the door. The car sped off into traffic. The two Koreans stood on the curb watching them leave.

***

The Korean representative observed his two henchmen watching the SUV with Li Ming disappear into traffic. He hurried over to where they stood. "We must grab her. She has vital information we need to complete our mission. Get her computer and notes. Do not harm her. Find out who the American representative is and eliminate him if he causes any trouble."

The two Koreans nodded their understanding and left the courtyard. The Korean representative took out his phone and punched a number. When the call was answered he spoke. "She is here and has been whisked away by the Americans in a black SUV. We need assistance in locating her. As soon as you locate her call me." He broke off off the call and spoke a few expletives.

The Korean representative was not a scientist but a high ranking operative of the RGB. His assignment was to get information on the device. Seok Dong-Suk would not take failure lightly.

As he ended the call, a drone left the top of an office building nearby and began seeking the black SUV. It was not hard, the traffic was thick and the SUV was stuck in trafic.

***

Li Ming was speechless. She had endured a lot in the past 24 hours. Now she was in a car with an FBI agent speeding away from a meeting that was obviously set up by the North Koreans to expose her experiments. Maybe they were behind the theft at the Lab. That also meant they had someone on the inside of the administration of Fudan University to arrange the symposium so quickly.

William Braun sat quietly and removed the faux beard. "Do you want to ask me any questions?"

"Yes, but first where are you taking me?" She was concerned and remembered what the chief of security had said a month ago. "*Don't trust even the government agents with information about your work*".

"We're headed to a safe place. The North Koreans have information about all of your friends and contacts here in Shanghai. They also have an agent in the University. So far they have not been successful in grabbing you. They could have killed you on several occasions, but they want you alive to help them with their test of your device. Yes, it was them that stole the device from your lab."

He turned and looked Li Ming in the eyes. "You were very lucky in the taxi accident. They underestimated your ability to avoid their man. Unfortunately one of our best agents was killed along with the taxi driver. I assume you are the one that phoned the police emergency and had the police check on your aunt. That was brilliant. Two of the Koreans were captured but are not cooperating with the police. For security reasons we have not informed the police about your where-abouts or what this is all about."

"I'm not sure what this is all about. Why are the North Koreans after my experiments? How on earth do they think they can use the device they stole to any advantage? I know you may not have all the answers, but I'm baffled by what has taken place and the cost in lives. This doesn't make sense."

The SUV turned off the Inter-Ring Road onto a wide four lane avenue. "Can you tell me where we are going? My aunt is expecting me to call this afternoon. I didn't have much of a breakfast and now no lunch. I am very hungry and feeling a bit ill."

"We are headed to a safe house in the western suburbs. We will be changing cars shortly. I don't think the North Koreans have enough resources to review every traffic camera in Shanghai, but we don't want to leave anything to chance." William reached into a bag in the back and took out a baseball cap and sweat shirt. "Put these on." Li Ming pulled on the sweat shirt and put on the cap. The car moved off the avenue to a side street with neat single family homes. It looked like any suburb in Pasadena. The car turned into a driveway. The driver pressed a button on the sun visor and the garage door went up.

Unnoticed, a drone dropped down behind a house across the street.

"Don't get out of the car yet. I will make arrangements for lunch and come to get you", said William.

Li Ming sat quietly in the back seat of the SUV. After about two minutes William came and opened her door. "It's safe to get out now."

Li Ming thought, *they don't even trust their own safe house.*

She was led into a comfortable home any family of well means would love. William motioned for her to seat herself at the dining room table. A Chinese woman came in with a try of steaming soup, sandwiches and a pot of tea. Li Ming was so hungry she didn't even wait for any introductions. She dug in and devoured the sandwiches and soup.

William spoke to two men; one was the driver of the SUV. The Chinese woman left the room and Li Ming thought she heard her doing something in the kitchen. She finished the soup and started to drink the tea. One of the men left the house. William and the SUV driver were in conversation when William's phone beeped. He stepped into another room to answer. Li Ming could not hear what was being said, it was just mumbling to her.

"We are ready to finish our journey", said William. "We are about an hour away. There may not be cell phone service, so I suggest you phone your aunt and explain you must be away for another night. Don't say anything else about what has happened in the past two days." Li Ming nodded and took out her phone.

"Aunt, this is Li Ming." She listened for several minutes. Tears came to her eyes. William saw she was getting emotional and motioned for the driver to follow him to another room. "Yes, it's been a long time. This trip is very important and I'm so sorry to have to tell you that I will not be able to come see you until possibly tomorrow." She listened to her aunt sob. It was breaking her heart not to be with her only living relative. "I promise. I'll call you as soon as I've finished my business. Good bye." She ended the call and wiped her eyes.

William and the driver returned to the dining room where Li Ming was sitting with her head down. "Is all okay?" asked William.

"Yes, I told her I'd call tomorrow."

"Good, we have to leave now." The driver opened the back door to the house. A different car was sitting in an alley behind the house. They got in and moved to the main street. William took out his phone and sent a text. Li Ming surmised it was to let someone know they were on their way to someplace.

Li Ming remembered her backpack was still at Zhon's dorm room.

"William, my back pack is in the dorm at the university. It has my personal items and clothes." William looked alarmed.

"Is there anything in the backpack about your work?"

"No only my personal stuff. I can call and have her store it for me until I can come by and pick it up. She was expecting me to come by this afternoon."

William was in thought. "Who knows you stayed with your friend last night?"

"First, I met her yesterday. Her brother helped me and offered to find me a place to spend the night. I never met them before yesterday. There is no connection to anyone or to any of my friends."

William looked relieved. "Great, before we lose cell service text her that you are staying with friends tonight and to hold on to your backpack until you call." Li Ming typed in the message and pressed the send button.

***

The street they turned into was thinly populated. It appeared many of the homes had been demolished for some reason. There were no cars parked along the street. A few were pulled into the front yards. They turned into what looked like a rundown old style house. The drone hid behind a low wall surounding a demolished old house across the street.

The car pulled into a shed that didn't have a door. The driver got out and went into the house from a rear door. In less than a minute he emerged and opened the door for William and Li Ming to exit. They went into the house using the rear door. The first thing Li Ming noticed was that the place appeared to have not been lived in for a very long time. Dust and broken furniture littered the main room. The kitchen did not have a cooker or fridge. She looked questionably at William. He was smiling. "Not to worry, it gets better."

Their driver pressed a few buttons on his phone and a kitchen cupboard began to turn. It opened to a dark stair case that went downward. William motioned for Li Ming to follow their driver down the staircase. At the bottom of the stairs was another door. When it opened the stairs was bathed in strong light. There was a whirring sound from above. The cupboard was returned to its position.

William guided her into a room with comfortable sofas and chairs. There was a flat screen TV. A Chinese woman appeared. She spoke to Li Ming in English. "Please be comfortable. May I get you something to drink or eat?"

"Oh, no thanks, I ate only a short time ago. What is this place?"

William sat and motioned for Li Ming to do the same. He motioned toward the Chinese woman and introduced her as Susan. "This is a safe house. It is used for extreme circumstances. All government agencies have one in every country. Susan is an agent for the CIA and is giving us the courteously of its use. The FBI has no safe house in Shanghai. The house I took you to for lunch belongs to an employee of the US Consulate office. Your case has been turned over to the CIA. You will be safe here and if you need anything, just ask Susan. You two will have a chat in a few moments."

Some of the terms William used in his conversation were not familiar to Li Ming. She had read some spy novels while in Pasadena but did not know much about how the spy business worked. She wondered about her own government. "Is the Chinese government aware of what is going on?"

Susan sat down. "We are not sure. We do know they were aware of the theft of your device by the North Koreans. Like us, they are baffled. I would guess they know you traveled to Shanghai yesterday. They may not know about the connection to the incident at the airport and the taxi accident." She looked over at William. "Our superiors are deciding at this moment about what to do about updating the MSS, the Chinese equivalent of the CIA. William if you will excuse us, I would like to speak to Li Ming privately." William nodded and left the room.

Li Ming sat very quietly. She reminded herself about what the chief of security had said about information. Susan got up and went into a small alcove and came back with a tray containing a pot of tea and some cookies. "Li Ming, the US government has sponsored your experiments for three full years. We are very pleased with the results. Our scientists at Area 51 have never experienced such dedication in one of their own as you have shown. I am not a scientist, but I do understand the principles of Quantum Mechanics and theoretical physics. I have read everything I can get my hands on about the infamous Philadelphia experiment in 1943. To be frank, I never thought it would be possible. I was briefed yesterday on the phone by Dr. March. He explained the breakthrough you made on the device. I am impressed."

Li Ming sat with her hands in her lap. She was not sure what to say. "Susan, just what did Dr. March tell you?"

"Well, as you might expect, it was mostly tech speak to me. But essentially he said that you had actually moved matter through the device and successfully retrieved it back in its identical form and proved it was the original with the small etching you placed on it for identification."

Li Ming raised her eyebrows. The only way Susan could have known about the etching was from Dr. March. It was his idea to make the etching to convince others it was indeed the same matter. Only she and Dr. March knew of the etching. "I'm very flattered you give me credit for solving one of nature's most complicated puzzles. I am just one of many that work on the Lotus Project." She looked down and reached for a cup of tea.

"I am trying to understand why the North Koreans are risking so much to get a device that is not anywhere near the stage to be of practical value", said Susan.

Li Ming wrinkled her brow. "Maybe they have been misled as to its capabilities. I agree, there is no practical use for the device at this time. Star Trek's beam me up Scotty scenario is so far in the future, most of us will be long gone by the time that is perfected, if ever."

Susan nodded her head affirming Li Ming's assessment of the device. "I think you may be onto something about being misled. Maybe someone or group has convinced the North Koreans that the device can be used to move troops or equipment without conventional methods. That would have a tremendous impact on the balance of military power. If the device could move weapons in an instant to anywhere on the globe, it would change the entire playing field."

Li Ming sat thinking. Her secret component was still her secret. None of the scientist knew of its importance, not even Dr. March. She alone had the key to the success or the failure of the device.

Susan said, "Dr. Wu, I must leave for a while. I will be back at dinner time and we can make plans to get you back to California."

Susan had been briefed only hours ago of an interception of top secret communications between a North Korean general and a leading scientist. In essence the conversation revealed the plan to use the stolen device to transmit nuclear devices into China and blackmail the world's powers into recognizing North Korea as the leader of the world. It sounded preposterous but worse things had been uttered by North Korea.

Chapter 5

Beijing, China

Jai Chun had three of his top agents in his office and he was very unhappy. The scientist, Dr. Wu was in Shanghai and they had no idea why. She had escaped their shadow from the University. The so called symposium was a sham, according to their University contact. It had been hastily arranged by a visiting North Korea professor. No one knew of the invitations until confirmations began to come into the administration office.

"We have a problem. The North Koreans have stolen something from a lab in Pasadena. They have set up a phony symposium at Fudan. They have agents running all over Shanghai looking for Dr. Wu. We do not know where she is or why she is here." He looked into the faces of his three agents. "I want to know what is going on. Each of us may be out of a job if we don't get a handle on this soon. Now get out of here and get me some answers."

The three agents made a hasty exit from Chun's office. His phone rang. He noted the caller ID indicated the call was from Shanghai. "This is Jai Chun." His eyebrow went up as he listened to someone. "Yes." Pause. "I'm not sure." Pause. "I can be in Shanghai in a couple of hours. Thank you." Chun put down the phone and sat with a very puzzled look on his face. *Why are the Americans involved in Dr. Wu's visit?*

Jai Chun had his secretary make arrangements for a private plane to take him to Shanghai immediately. He did not include his three agents. They had their job sorting out what the other agents had discovered in Pasadena and Shanghai. He phoned the office of the President. He was surprised when he was put straight through. "Mr. President, this is Jai Chun. I have been called to Shanghai for a meeting with the American CIA. They claim to have intelligence that is vital to our country. We shall see. I will not be able to brief you until I return." He listened to the President for a few seconds. "Yes sir, I will call you before I leave Shanghai with a verbal report."

Shanghai

The plane ride to Shanghai was uneventful. Jai Chun made several calls. One of the calls was to his chief agent in Shanghai. All the agent could tell him was that Dr. Wu vanished from the University. His people lost her immediately after the symposium had adjourned for lunch. They had not been allowed into the building where the meeting was taking place. They guessed at which entrance she would emerge and were wrong.

The plane landed and taxied to a hanger far from the main terminal. Two agents greeted Chun and took him to a car. "Sir, where would you like to go?" asked one of the agents.

"Take me to our office. I want a meeting with all department heads as soon as we arrive." The agent took out his phone and relayed the order to someone at the MSS's office in Shanghai.

***

Jai Chun entered the elevator of a modern office building in downtown Shanghai. The MSS owned the building and were occupying it as an insurance company. A special card was required to make the elevator stop on the eighth floor. When the door opened he was greeted by his agent-in-charge who led the way to the conference room already occupied by several people standing waiting for their boss.

"People, please sit. We have some urgent business to discuss." Most in the room had never met Jai Chun and were in awe of his presence. "A citizen of Shanghai, Dr. Wu Li Ming has returned from America. She is a very important scientist working on a project for the US government. Her work is highly classified and even I have no idea what it may be. We know that the North Koreans stole a device from her lab at Cal Tech in Pasadena, California. We know the North Koreans set up a bogus symposium at Fudan University to lure her here. We do not know why. It is your job to find out everything about the device they stole, why Dr. Wu is so important and most importantly, identify the North Korean agents." He looked each person in the eye. "Now get out of here and find some answers."

The agents quickly left the conference room. His agent-in-charge was nervous. He knew that his office should have known what this was about. He didn't have a clue and had never heard of Dr. Wu.

Jai Chun motioned for his agent to sit down. "Li, we have to get a handle on what the North Koreans are up to. I have to meet a CIA agent in half an hour. They have some information that may or may not impact this case with the North Koreans. I was told that there may be a foreign threat here in Shanghai. I don't know much more. The CIA may be playing a game, but it is highly unusual for them to be so abrupt in calling a meeting without any preamble. They usually send us messages with information and then meet to explain. This time it was a phone call and no real information." He sat back and watched the face of his agent-in-charge.

"Sir, where is the meeting to take place?"

"They want to meet here." The agent jumped as if he sat on an electric wire.

"Sir that is unheard of. Maybe it is a ruse to get into our office. How many are coming?" Sweat formed on the agent's forehead.

"Only one female agent is coming. Our agency responsible for keeping track of foreign operatives has no picture of her or even knows who she is. She identified herself as Susan Daley. We have zero information on any CIA operative named Susan Daley and our American agents have no information on her either. I want our office to be on alert, but we must show her all the courtesy we can show. This will be a first."

***

At half past four in the afternoon, Susan Daley entered the Pacific Indemnity Insurance office. She went to the reception desk in the lobby and asked to see Mr. Jai Chun. The receptionist phoned someone. Within a minute the elevator doors opened to the lobby. A well dressed man approached Susan. "I am Mr. Leong. I will take you to Mr.

Jai Chun." Susan nodded without comment and followed him into the waiting elevator. The man put a card into the slot for the eighth floor.

The door opened to a large room with many cubicles. It could have been any floor in the CIA headquarters in Virginia. Mr. Leong led Susan through a maze of busy workers typing on computer keyboards. The conference room was medium size and seated at the head was Jai Chun.

"Ms Daley, I am Jai Chun, we spoke on the phone. Please have a seat." Chun was surprised Ms. Daley appeared to be Asian not American, he had spoken in broken English. It was obvious that English would be a struggle.

"Mr. Chun we can converse in Mandarin. Since I called this meeting, I would like to suggest we have someone to record our conversation so there will be no misunderstandings. I think you will see why after we begin." Chun nodded and motioned for Mr. Leong to make the arrangements. He left the room.

"Ms Daley, this is a total surprise. I don't think our two organizations have ever sat down to talk in the same room. I am honored. are your parens Chinese." He smiled and appeared to relax.

Susan smiled, "Yes, I was born in Hong Kong. My father worked for the United States Navy. He was transferred back to the US when I was three years old."

A middle aged woman came into the room with a small recording device and placed it on the table in front of Jai Chun. She pressed the record button and nodded, turned and closed the door behind her leaving only Susan and Jai in the room. Susan leaned forward.

"What I'm about to tell you may sound like a soap opera, but we believe the North Koreans are planning to make a military move against China." Jai Chun was visibly stunned with that statement. He had no evidence from his people that North Korea had the capability or the expertise to launch such a plan.

"Ms. Daley, that is preposterous. North Korea is an ally of China. What evidence do you have of such a charge?"

"Jai, we have evidence the North Koreans have stolen a very radical piece of equipment that may be capable of transporting weapons to any place on earth instantly. We think they may be planning to experiment with the device using China as the testing platform."

Jai Chun sat very quiet and listened carefully to Susan speak. He knew of the stolen device. He knew the North Koreans had an interest in Dr. Wu. He knew that Dr. Wu had disappeared from the symposium. He knew the meeting was an elaborate ruse to get Dr. Wu to come to China. What he didn't know was why. Now the CIA is telling him the North Koreans are planning some military action against China. This was too farfetched to believe.

"Ms Daley, China has one of the most powerful military forces in the world. The North Koreans have a large force but nothing compared to our overwhelming army. It is not possible they would attempt an action against us. We could take them out in a matter of hours."

"Jai we do not think they will use conventional means. If they can get the stolen device to work, they could transmit nuclear devices to any spot or multiple locations within China. You would be totally unaware of where the devices are located and defenseless to disarm them." Susan saw the wrinkles appear as she spoke. He was absorbing the enormous danger his country was in.

"What evidence do you have that they plan to do this to China? I find it amusing that if they could transmit the nuclear devices anywhere on the globe, they would pick their neighbor to do so."

"We think they picked China because they must confirm the device works and the nuclear bombs are in place. They can easily do that with the ease of crossing the border with agents to check on each location. Once they have confirmed that the device worked, they will blackmail the world powers to surrender. We also think there is something wrong with their plan. We know they have had the device for over a month. We do not believe they have been successful in making it work. That is why they need Dr. Wu. She can make it work. Every effort should be made to stop their plan and get the device back. They tried to grab her at the International airport two days ago. One person was killed. They attempted to kidnap her in a taxi from the airport. She escaped but the driver and one other person was killed in the attempt. Yesterday two North Koreans were arrested by the Shanghai police for kidnapping a bookshop owner who just happens to be the only living relative of Dr. Wu. Today, they tried to grab her at Fudan University. We had people in place and were able to rescue her before the North Korean agents. We have people watching Dr. Wu's aunt. We think there will be another attempt to grab the aunt and force Dr. Wu to do their bidding." Susan's phone beeped. She knew it had to be an emergency. She looked at the number. It was from her office. "I'm sorry but I have to take this. Jai Chun nodded but kept seated.

Susan got up from the table and went to the farthest corner of the room. "Yes this is Susan. She listened. "Are you sure? How many down? She turned pale at the answer. "I will be back in an hour." She punched off the call and walked slowly to her seat.

"Ms Daley is everything ok?" asked Jai Chun.

"No, the North Koreans have raided our safe house and kidnapped Dr. Wu. Four of my agents are down. The aunt has also been kidnapped. Three of my agents there are down. I need your help." She looked very vulnerable.

Jai Chun was very shocked. The Americans had agents running all over Shanghai and none of his people had clue what was happening. This is going to be very embarrassing. "Ms Daley, I am terribly sorry for your loss. I will do what I can. Please remain here for a few minutes as I gather my staff and brief them on the situation." Susan nodded.

Jai Chun got up and left the room. He closed the door behind him. He was very concerned. He went straight to his chief agent's office. He closed the door. "Lu, the Americans have four agents down. Dr. Wu has been kidnapped along with her aunt. I want a task force pulled together now. I will give you instructions after I complete my meeting with the CIA agent. Call the Shanghai police. Find out what they know about an incident at the airport yesterday, a taxi crash with two bodies that had been shot and the arrest of two North Korean agents at a bookstore n Pudong." The agent sat still with his mouth open. Nothing came out. "Do nothing beyond getting the information from the police. Do not tip the police as any connection between the incidents." Jai Chun got up and left the office and returned to the conference room.

"Ms Daley, I have ordered my agent in charge to prepare a task force but do nothing until we have a plan." Susan noted the 'we'.

"Thank you Jai." She sat for a few minutes thinking. "I don't think

Dr. Wu's life is in danger at the moment. The North Koreans are going to attempt to get Dr. Wu out of China and into North Korea. I think you should alert the border crossings to be very through in their searches of vehicles crossing. As for the aunt, I don't think they would take the chance on moving her to North Korean. I think they will hold her here and put the pressure on Dr. Wu to make their device work."

"Yes, I agree with all you have said." He picked up the phone on the table and called in his chief agent.

"Lu, I want you to dispatch a cleanup team to the bookshop. Canvas the neighborhood for any chance someone saw something unusual this afternoon. If the police show up call me." Lu nodded his head and left the room. "Your safe house that was raided, where is it?"

Susan wrote the address down on one of the pads at each of the positions around the table. "My team has sanitized the location, but I can give you codes to the security system if you wish."

"That won't be necessary. I'm sure your people have everything under control. Just how many people do you have in Shanghai? He grinned not expecting an answer.

Susan grinned back. How many do you have in Washington?" They both laughed. It felt good to have a bit of humor break the dismal situation. "I will have a report from my people and I will share any information that can help catch up with Dr. Wu or her aunt. I must get back to my office now." She got up and extended her hand to Jai Chun. He accepted it with a smile.

They each had a lot of work to do and not much information to go on. Jai Chun had one of the hardest things to do that he had ever done as head of the MSS, he had to phone the President and brief him on the situation. He may not have a job afterwards.

Chapter 6

CIA Safe House

Li Ming sat in the safe house's lounge area. She felt like a prisoner. There was not much on TV and the two guards were silent. The woman Susan said she would be back in time for dinner and would bring her up to date on all that was happening. A soft bump came from the floor above. One of the guards took out his phone and punched in a series of numbers. He listened but no one answered. He immediately jumped up and told the other guard to get their guest into the hard room.

The second guard came over and motioned for Li Ming to follow him. She was getting up when loud gun shots rang out. Her guard slumped to the floor. The second guard came running in and was gunned down before he could draw his weapon. A man in a ski mask stood at the door that led up to the kitchen. He came and checked all the rooms. He yelled something in Korean and four men and a woman dressed in dark clothes and each wearing ski masks ran down the steps and into the room. The woman had a cloth tote bag.

She spoke in Mandarin for Li Ming to sit down in one of the chairs. Li Ming nodded and sat down. One of the men checked the bodies of the two guards. They were defiantly dead. Li Ming knew the group was North Korean.

The woman walked over and leaned down to face Li Ming. "Be quiet and behave and you won't get hurt." She removed a wig and sweater from the tote and ordered Li Ming to put them on. Li Ming struggled to get the sweater over her head but was assisted by the woman. She put the wig over her short hair. The wig was long black hair. The woman took out a roll of gray duct tape from the tote and taped Li Ming's hands together.

One of the men spoke into his phone. He nodded at the woman. The woman grabbed Li Ming under the arm and made her stand. "If you make any noise I will shoot you." She stared into Li Ming's eyes. She pushed Li Ming to the steps and up to the kitchen. Two of the other CIA agents were lying on the floor. They were dead. The woman pushed Li Ming toward the back door and out to a waiting van. One of the men got in and started the engine. Li Ming was pushed into the back seat, with the woman sitting beside her. The other men left in a car waiting in the front yard of the house.

They had not searched Li Ming when they bound her hands. She still had her phone tucked into her jeans pocket. She remembered that there was no cell service but the North Koreans had used their phones, so there must be service. She had to get to her phone and alert the authorities. *I don't know anyone's phone number. The only numbers I have are to Zhon and my aunt. Not good.*

The van jostled as it ran over some railroad tracks. Li Ming could see out the front windshield, but the scene was totally foreign to her. They were in some industrial complex. Large buildings with cranes and huge doors that had train tracks going under them. It must be a train repair station. The van came to a stop. The woman sat still until the driver got out and checked on something behind a normal size door. He motioned for them to go into the building.

The woman jerked on Li Ming's arm and pulled her from the van. "Ow, that hurt." The woman didn't respond. *This is insane.*

The building was large. There were several railroad cars in the building, but no workers. It looked as if it had been abandoned. She was pushed toward a door that appeared to be an office. One of the men opened the door and the woman guided her into a small room with a desk and chairs and was pushed into one of the chairs. The duct tape was removed from her wrists. The sticky stuff pulled some skin from her arms. The driver of her van pulled her arms behind her and duct taped her hands behind the chair. Li Ming gritted her teeth. She gulped air and a tear came. All of the Koreans left the room and closed the door. *No guard? What do they want with me? Surely they don't think I can help with the device in this place.*

Several minutes went by. The door opened and two well dressed men entered. She recognized one as the North Korean representative to the faux symposium. The representative walked up to her and leaned down. "You will now tell us about the experiments you have been conducting at Cal Tech." He stood up. Li Ming looked him in the eye but said nothing.

"Well, you seem to be lost for words. I'm sure your aunt will not like that." He took out his phone and pressed a button. The phone was not a normal cell phone but one of the satellite types. He spoke in Korean and put the phone up to Li Ming's ear. She heard her aunt crying and begging Li Ming to do whatever they want. The North Korean took the phone away and spoke several words in Korean before shutting off the call. "As you can hear, your aunt is fine, for now. If you don't cooperate then things may change for her."

Li Ming was devastated. Her aunt's life was in her hands. She had to do what they wanted. She had witnessed their total lack of concern for human life. "What do you want me to do? I can't do anything here in this place. The equipment needed is not here." She looked at the North Korean for an explanation. The man's face was set in a smirk and he turned and left the room. The other man who had not spoken remained. She was not sure what they were going to do. So many people had died because of her. Her aunt's life was at stake. She was distraught. Tears came to her and she sobbed. The man standing at the door showed no emotion. His face was like a plastic mask.

Chapter 7

Unknown Area Northwest of Shanghai

The man standing guard had his back against the door. A knock made him turn and open the door just wide enough for him to see who was knocking. He pulled the door fully open. It was the woman that had ridden here in the van. She smiled and pulled one of the chairs to sit in front of Li Ming.

"You will be transported to another location shortly. Keep the wig on. If you make any noise or try to escape your aunt will pay the consequences. Is that clear?" She stared into Li Ming's eyes waiting for a response. Li Ming nodded yes. "Good, we will be leaving shortly." The woman stood and moved the chair back against the far wall. The door opened and the man that had been at the fake symposium came in and spoke in a whisper to the woman. Li Ming understood no Korean even if she could have heard the conversation. The man left the room.

The guard cut the duct tape that was holding her hands behind her. He made a motion for her to stand. Obviously he did not speak Mandarin. Li Ming stood and the woman took her by the arm and moved her through the door to a waiting van. This van was different and had plain windows, not blocked with some dark material.

The side door was open and the woman told Li Ming to sit in the seat on the opposite side. She climbed in and took her seat. The woman took the seat beside her and told her to buckle her seat belt. The guard took the front passenger's seat. The van pulled out and crossed several open areas with huge pot holes filled with water. There were no other cars or trucks to be seen. This place was definitely off the main roads.

***

Several hours went by. She had nodded off twice. It was now very dark outside. The van slowed and pulled into a well lit service area. The driver pulled up to the fuel pumps and got out. He filled the tank and went into the building. In a few minutes he returned. He started the van and resumed the drive. The highway was surprisingly full of traffic, mostly trucks and vans. Li Ming noticed that their van was similar to the dozens that were on the road. They would not stand out. It was getting dark and many of the vehicles had on their headlights. Li Ming asked the woman if they were going to a hotel for the night. The woman just smiled and shook her head no. Li Ming had calculated in her head that the fuel stop had occurred at least four hours after their departure from the safe house.

Li Ming saw the clock on the dashboard. It read 7:15. Based on the distance the van could cover on one tank of fuel, she figured they would be stopping again after 1a.m. for more fuel. She nodded off again.

When she woke, she saw that it was 12:30. They would be stopping shortly if she was correct in her calculations. The distance from Shanghai to the North Korean boarder was nearly 1,500 miles. Surely they would not drive straight through. She saw a sign that had several cities printed with the distance. One was Ganyu, near a sea port. The distance was 60 Kilometers. Maybe they were going to transfer to a boat. The woman startled her when she spoke to the driver. He motioned to the clock and said something back. Li Ming did not understand the words, but she guessed the driver was telling the woman they would arrive at some place shortly.

The van went through Ganyu without stopping. Li Ming saw a sign with the outline of a plane. The distance said 10K. She thought maybe they were going to an airport. The guard took out his phone and made a call. He spoke several minutes and hung up, then turned to the woman and spoke several words and then turned back. The van reached an intersection and turned off to the right. Li Ming saw a sign on the far side of the intersection with the outline of the plane and 2K. They were not going to the airport. The road became very bumpy and full of pot holes.

The van turned left onto a road that was not hard surfaced. They drove for a few minutes at a very slow pace. The guard pointed at something ahead, but Li Ming could only see shadows. The van stopped. A man came out from the trees and spoke with the driver, then waved him through. He did not wear a uniform but had a gun slung over his shoulder. There was light ahead, showing what Li Ming thought were large barns. The van pulled around the first building and the door opened, and the van drove into the building. There were four or five men with guns standing near the door. The woman told Li Ming to sit without speaking and not to move. One of the men with some sort of automatic weapon came up to the van and pulled open the door next to the woman. She climbed out and walked a few meters away with the man. He seemed agitated for some reason. They stood talking for a few minutes. The driver and the guard remained in the van.

The woman came back to the van and spoke to the driver and the guard. They did not seem pleased with what she told them. "Dr. Wu, there has been a delay in our departure. We will be staying here for about six hours for our transportation to arrive. You may get out and use our facilities." Li Ming nodded and removed the seat belt and climbed down from the van. The woman walked with her to a small office area that had a restroom. The woman remained outside the door.

Li Ming pulled her iPhone out and noted that there was no signal, bummer. She tucked the phone back in her jeans. When she came out of the restroom, the woman and the guard were standing waiting. The guard motioned for her to follow him into the office while the woman used the facilities. There were several chairs and desks and each desk had a computer. There was a sofa against one wall. Li Ming looked longingly at the sofa. She would give anything to lie down for an hour or so. So much had happened in the last 24 hours; she really could not believe the mess she was in.

The guard motioned for her to sit in the chair in front of one of the desks. He did not tape her hands this time. The woman came in and spoke to the guard. He left and closed the door. "Li Ming, please use the sofa to get some sleep. It will be a long time before you will have another opportunity." Li Ming nodded and stretched out on the sofa. She fell asleep almost immediately.

***

The noise of a plane's engine woke her. She was alone in the office. The door opened and one of the men with an automatic weapon came in. "Please follow me." He spoke Mandarin. She got up and followed him to a room next to the office. There was a long table full of food and steaming hot tea. She looked at the man. "Am I allowed to eat some of the food?" He nodded and motioned for her to sit. The food was delicious. She was very hungry. The woman came in and smiled at her. She helped herself to the food and tea. They ate in silence.

Two uniformed men came in and ate. She was curious as to who they were. That mystery was solved almost before she could think about it. The woman spoke to the men. They turned and stared at Li Ming. "These men are your pilots and will take you to your destination. I will be going with you." She sat down and sipped her tea.

The pilots finished their meal and spoke to the woman. She nodded. "We will board the plane now. Please follow me." They left the building and Li Ming saw a large plane parked with the door open and the steps down. She followed the woman up the stairs and into the plane. It was not a passenger plane. It appeared to be a cargo plane. There were no airline type seats. Two makeshift seats had been made against the fuselage.

"Please sit and buckle in." Li Ming sat down. The seat was not much more than a piece of canvas stretched between aluminum pipes. She sat and found the seat belt. She wondered why bother, if there was much turbulence the entire seat would come loose. The door banged shut and the pilots closed the door between the cargo area and the cockpit. The engines revived up and they taxied to a dirt strip. The sun was just coming over the horizon and Li Ming could see the sea. It was shining red and orange from the first rays of the sun. Large container vessels were dotted about. The plane began to move down the runway. There were bumps and turns that were made to dodge the pot holes. The plane lifted off the ground and skimmed along the water toward North Korea. Li Ming felt she could almost touch the water they were flying so low. She figured it was in order to be under the Chinese radar.

Chapter 8

Somewhere in North Korea

The plane ride was rough. Air turbulence caused the plane to bump and swiay in alarming ways. Being so close to the water was nerve racking enough, but the constant jarring made both passengers look at each other. There was no doubt this was not an everyday occurrence for the woman accompanying Li Ming.

The trip took about three hours before land appeared below them. The plane climbed to a higher altitude and the ride became smooth. The door opened from the cockpit. One of the pilots spoke to the woman and closed the door. The woman turned to Li Ming. "We will be landing in about twenty minutes." She smiled.

Li Ming wondered why the woman was appearing to befriend her. Maybe they would release her aunt. There was no indication of hostility from the woman or the two pilots. The engine began to change pitch and the plane began to descend. The woman checked their seat belts in preparation for landing. There were buildings dotting the landscape. A city came within view and the plane made a turn to the right. "What is the name of the city below?"

"We are landing at Songnim. It is a special zone. The entire city was built only two years ago. It was modeled after a small USA city, like the ones on TV shows. This is where you will stay and work." Li Ming nodded but asked no further questions.

The plane made a smooth landing. The airport building looked very modern and clean. Li Ming saw two SUV's parked in front of a hanger building. The plane headed in that direction. Three people were standing near the cars. One was a woman. The plane stopped and the engines were turned off. The door was opened by one of the pilots and he disembarked. Li Ming could hear him speaking to one of the men. The men and woman wore normal street clothes, with no guns in view.

The pilot came back in the plane and spoke to the woman passenger. She smiled and turned to Li Ming. "You will be taken to your residence and can rest for now. Tomorrow you will be taken to your lab. Please unbuckle and deplane." Li Ming unbuckled her seat belt and went down the steps to the tarmac. The woman stayed on the plane. One of the men came over and spoke to Li Ming in Mandarin. "My name is Jinho Pak and this is your assistant, Dauen Kim.", pointing at the waiting young woman. The woman came forward and shook Li Ming's hand.

"Dr. Wu, please follow me and we will go to your accommodations." She bowed slightly and motioned Li Ming to follow her to the lead car. They climbed in. Jinho Pak got in the driver's seat. The other man got into the other car. The cars moved onto a road beside the huge hanger. In the distance was a check point. Armed guards stood at attention as the two cars moved past the already raised barrier.

"Dr. Wu, we will go to a shopping mall to purchase you clothing. You are about my size and there should be no problem finding your new wardrobe. I noticed that you wear American jeans. They are rare here and I would suggest you replace them for the accepted outer wear." Li Ming nodded she understood. "Dr. Wu, Please call me Dauen. I am assigned to you. Whatever you need, I will do my best to obtain. I will be staying in the same accommodations and will accompany you to work."

Li Ming had a very serious look on her face. "Dauen, why am I here?

"I don't know anything about your circumstances. I was told that I was selected to be your companion because I graduated in theoretical physics. I have no idea what you are working on. I live a long way from here. My husband and two children are not sure when I will return." Jinho Pak looked up into the mirror. He made sure that Dauen saw his slight shake of the head to stop talking. They sat in silence for ten minutes.

The car pulled up to a large building with an awning extending out over the wide footpath. A tall man in a uniform opened the car door. Dauen motioned for Li Ming to follow her inside. The driver got out and spoke to the uniformed man. The man spoke into a portable radio. A door opened and a young man ran out and drove off in the SUV.

They walked into a large lobby that could have been any hotel in any country. Dauen went to the desk and presented an envelope to the desk clerk. The clerk opened the envelope and removed several documents. She turned and put the documents into a copy machine and returned the originals to the envelope and handed it back to Dauen. The clerk entered information into the computer on her desk. She took two key cards from a stack and swiped them through a device on the side of her monitor and then placed them on the counter. Dauen signed a document and took the key cards. "Okay, we are on the second level and our rooms connect. Let's inspect our rooms then we will go shopping." Li Ming saw Jinho Pak also check in as they moved to the bank of lifts. She also wondered where Dauen's luggage was. Surely they had plenty of time to make arrangements.

The lift was like new. It went noiselessly up to the second level. The two rooms were on the left down the hall a few doors from the lift. Dauen used one of the keys to open the first door. She pushed open the door and motioned for Li Ming to enter. The room was very modern and had two sofas, several large upholstered chairs and a work desk. There was an alcove with a dining table for six. The bedrooms were on either side of the main room. That gave a lot of privacy. "You pick the bedroom", said Dauen.

Li Ming looked at the bedroom on the right then the left one. "They seem to be identical. I'll take the one on the right." Dauen nodded and started toward the bedroom on the left when a knock at the door stopped her. She went to the door and a man with several large luggage bags entered. Dauen spoke to him. He nodded and went to the bedroom on the left with the luggage. That solved one of Li Ming's questions. The man left and Dauen went into her room and closed the door.

In a few minutes she returned. Li Ming was seated on one of the sofas. "Let's go get you some clothes." There was a phone on the desk. Dauen picked up the hand piece and punched in several numbers. She spoke only a few words and replaced the phone. "The car will be around to take us to the shopping mall. Are you ready?"

"Yes."

The ride to the mall was short. The mall was not the type Li Ming expected. It was not like in Shanghai or the USA. The mall consisted of many small vendor stands in what looked like a long alley. They exited the car and Dauen led Li Ming through the maze of stalls and shops that opened into a large courtyard that contained a small park with rides for kids. Several mothers with small ones were on the rides.

"Dauen, is this a typical shopping area?"

"Yes, most of the people shop after work. Only a few who are on special care can come during the day. The mall is open until midnight."

"What is special care?"

"A mother with more than two kids is awarded a stipend to stay at home and care for the small ones. Having more than two children is encouraged. Here is the store with women's clothing." She pushed open the door. Bells above the door tinkled announcing their arrival.

A middle aged woman came from behind a rack of coats and spoke to Dauen. Dauen motioned towards Li Ming and must have explained what she needed. The woman looked at Li Ming. She spoke to Dauen and motioned towards the back of the shop. "The shop keeper wants to show you some special clothes that she thinks you will like." The three walked to the back of the shop.

The clothes were very plain, but fit Li Ming. They purchased three outfits, under garments, a pair of shoes and a heavy coat and hat. Dauen took an envelope from her pocket and presented it to the clerk. The clerk read the document and wrote some numbers on a space. She handed the document back to Dauen who signed it and passed it back. Li Ming guessed it was like a check or voucher of some kind.

The shop keeper put all the purchases into a large cloth tote bag. Dauen picked up the bag and they left the shop. It had been several hours since Li Ming had eaten. She saw a vendor stand across the park. She turned to Dauen, "Can we buy some food? I ate a long time ago."

"Of course, there are several places to eat. What would you like?"

"Dim Sum would be great" said Li Ming. Dauen smiled and pointed to a café.

"The food here may be different than you are accustomed to, but it is good." They walked across the green park to the café. There were five tables and only one open. They took their seats. The menu was in Korean, so Dauen explained each of the dishes. Li Ming listened and picked two items. A waiter came and Dauen ordered for the two.

Li Ming looked around the café. There did not appear to be any-one interested in them. There were no guards with guns. She knew that to run or hide would not accomplish anything. She didn't speak the language, know the geographic location and had no money. She was stuck. Her aunt was constantly on her mind. She needed to know that she was not harmed. An idea was forming.

Chapter 9

Shanghai

Susan Daley walked to the corner from the MSS building. A Toyota SUV stopped and she got in. There were two men in the front, both Asian. The car pulled into traffic and headed north. No one spoke. The car eventually turned into an underground garage. A large metal door came down after the car entered. Three men stood near the bank of lifts. They were alert and stood at attention.

Susan's door was opened by one of the men. He bowed slightly and helped her out. The two men in the front seats remained in the car. The lift door opened and Susan entered. One of the men joined her and punched a button for the sixth floor. The man took out a small radio and spoke several words. Susan was not paying attention. She had a lot of things on her mind. The families of the agents killed had to be notified. The bodies had to be taken to the airport for transport to the States. The American embassy had to be notified of the incident. She had to file a detailed report to Langley. She had to begin to make plans on how to get Dr. Wu back to California. Jai Chun would help, she was sure.

***

Jai Chun terminated the dreaded call to his President. He sat back in his chair and reviewed all that was said. He had not mentioned the theory of the North Koreans using their stolen device to plant nuclear devices throughout China. In fact, he did not believe that theory and felt that Susan Daley was not completely convinced either. The President was not critical of what had happened. He had listened to every detail and then asked Jai what plans had been made to investigate the incidents.

Jai Chun explained that the American CIA and the Chinese MSS were working together to find out what this was all about. No Chinese citizen had been harmed and none seemed to be involved, the woman killed at the airport was Japanese. The bookshop owner was the exception and would be priority in the investigation. The President accepted Jai's plan to work with the Americans and asked to be updated each morning. A knock on the door brought Jai out of his concentration. "Yes, come in."

"Sir, I have the reports from the police. The incident at the airport involved one woman passenger from Japan being killed. The shooter was killed by the security guards. He had no ID. He was not Chinese. It all took place in the arrivals hall as passengers deplaned from a flight from Los Angeles. No one else was harmed. The taxi crash with two bodies that had been shot is still being investigated. No one seems to know anything. There was a rumor that a woman passenger got out of the taxi and left the scene. The book store reported two North Korean men attempted to rob the store. The shop keeper was not harmed and the police arrived before they could escape. She is the aunt of Dr. Wu. Her name is Wang lui."

"Thank you. Did you get a report on the CIA safe-house situation?"

"No sir, our people are still there. I will report back when they have completed their investigation." The agent left Jai's office.

Jai had confirmed that Susan Daley's report was true and accurate. He felt he could trust her to be forthcoming with any new information. They had to get a handle on the kidnapping of Dr. Wu's aunt. If they could get her back, then the North Koreans would have no leverage over Dr. Wu. He still could not accept that a young woman from Shanghai could be involved in such a huge scientific endeavor. *Women should not be placed into such positions that require a man's strength and understanding. Chinese traditions are eroding.* The new women's rights movement was not something Jai could accept.

Jai picked up his phone and punched in a number. "Come to my office and bring your two best agents." He put the phone down and rubbed his hands over his smooth face. He was making a plan. Someone had to have seen something at the bookshop. The knock on the door announced the arrival of his men to start unraveling this situation.

***

Susan Daley entered a conference room with several people seated around a large table. "As most of you know, we have lost several of our agents and friends. The situation is dire. There appears to be a plot by the North Koreans to destabilize the world with threats of nuclear consequences. Our job is to find out what the plot involves, who is in charge, locate Dr. Wu and her aunt. The MSS has pledged to assist; after all it is their country. I don't think they believe the threat they are under. Jai Chun is a conservative man that believes in the old Chinese traditions. Therefore, it will be left to us to expose the plot and convince Jai of the threat." Hands went up. A young Chinese woman raised her hand. "Yes Joan."

"Ms Daley, do we have any assets in North Korea to help in this investigation?" She looked around the table. Most of her colleagues just stared at the table top.

"Joan, that information is on a need to know basis. Your job is to find the aunt. Others will concentrate on finding Dr. Wu." Joan nodded and accepted Susan's statement.

"Let's start by going over the evidence at the safe house. I know there is not much, but run down every clue no matter how insignificant it is. A man raised his hand at the other end of the table.

"Yes." Susan did not know his name. He had been working in Beijing and was new to the Shanghai staff.

"Ms Daley, I am Nu Lee, it is highly likely that Dr. Wu was air lifted out of China and into North Korea. Can the Chinese supply us radar information?"

"Thank you Nu. If they used an airplane to move her to North Korea, find out the most likely location they could sneak a plane through the radar network. Also, check with anyone at the Beijing office that can supply us a lead to North Korean operatives that may be involved in a kidnapping of this magnitude." The man gave Susan a slight nod and got up and left the room.

"If any of you have any thoughts about any techniques to flush out the North Koreans, please share them as soon as possible." Susan dismissed the group to begin the task of finding Dr. Wu and her aunt. Her job now was to make the arrangements for the downed officers and prepare reports to her superiors in Langley.

***

Nu Lee went to his cubical. He logged onto the secret CIA network and sent an encrypted message to his former office in Beijing. After sending the message, he brought up a detailed map of the area north of Shanghai and along the sea coast. There were several medium sized towns but no large cities. He needed a map showing the radar installations and their range of search. He fired off another encrypted message to a different office. Within ten minutes he was rewarded with a message with an attachment. He had to run the attachment through the decoding software. It revealed a detailed map showing the radar installations. Each had a fan shaped pattern extending out over the water. Based on what he was seeing, each of the radar sites overlapped the other. There were no apparent gaps. He had not heard from his first message.

He was concentrating on the map when a thought occurred, what if there had been a power failure and one of the sites had been dark. He needed to know the sites without backup generators. It would not take much to bring down the power grid in the countryside. It would take several hours for crews to find the break and repair it. There would be plenty of time for a plane to enter and leave undetected. Nu got up from his cubical and walked to the end of the room. A middle aged man sat in front of a computer screen.

"Lum, can you find out if there were any power outages along the coast line north of Shanghai in the last 24 hours?" Lum looked up and smiled.

"Funny you should ask, I just received information that there was an explosion yesterday at a power substation near Ganyu. It is a small town on the coast. They got it back up and running about an hour ago."

"Thanks Lum." Nu went back to his cubical and typed another encrypted message. Within five minutes an answer came back. There were two radar sites that had no backup generators. They were located at abandoned air fields near Ganyu that were WWII vintage. Xia closed up his computer and went to Susan's office.

"Ms Daley may I have a moment?" Susan looked up from her computer and saw the man she had only met an hour ago.

"Nu, yes come in. What can I do for you?"

"Ms Daley, I may have a clue as to where Dr. Wu was taken to meet an airplane. There are several abandoned WWII airfields near a town named Ganyu. I need two or three drones to canvas the area for possible landing sights." Susan raised her eyebrows.

"Nu, have a seat. I think I can make those arrangements." She picked up her phone and consulted a card file. She punched in a number and waited. In perfect Mandarin, "May I speak to Jai Chun, this is Susan Daley." Nu was shocked she called the head of the MSS directly.

"Jai, Susan. I think we may have a lead and I need your help." She listened for several seconds. "We believe we have found out how the North Koreans sneaked a plane into China undetected and left with Dr. Wu." She listened again. "We think there is a connection between a power outage near Ganyu, a small town north of here and the radar network. We would like two or three drones to canvas the area for workable air fields that could have been used to take Dr. Wu to North Korea."

***

Jai was pleased with Susan's request. He was now directly involved in the investigation. He made arrangements for a helicopter to take him and three drone operators to Ganyu along with one of Susan's operatives.

Jai's driver took him to a special airfield near the western suburbs of Shanghai. It was small but could accommodate small jets and helicopters. Nu Lee was waiting for the arrival of the MSS group. He had been told to wait in the guard house at the main gate. Jai's car arrived and the guard told Jai that a man was waiting in the guard house for him. Nu came out and met Jai Chun and the three drone pilots. They shook hands. Nu got into Jai's car and they were taken to a hanger where they boarded a large Chinese Army helicopter. The trip took slightly less than two hours. They landed at an Army base near Ganyu. The drone pilots unloaded their gear and set up in one of the Army buildings. Jai and Nu watched as the team assembled all the equipment. Nu took this opportunity to explain his theory of how the radar could be disabled long enough to get a plane in and out of China at this location. The flight time from Ganyu and the interior of North Korea was about three hours.

The pilots announced they were ready. They all studied a map of the area. Jai suggested where each of the drones should cover. They would start the search at the damaged power substation and fan out from there. In forty-five minutes one of the pilots motioned for Jai and Nu take a look at his screen. At the end of an old abandoned road was an air field. The drone flew over the area. There were signs of recent usage from the tire marks in the mud. One of the buildings seemed to be usable. Nu asked the pilot to go near the buildings. The drone made a pass and one of the doors opened. Two men with sub machine guns emerged and looked up at the drone as it passed and flew off toward the sea.

Jai slapped Nu on the back. "That looks like their base of operations." He spoke to one of the pilots to phone the commander of the Army base and get a team to the air field as soon as possible. He told the pilot to keep the drone as far away as possible without losing the picture.

Nu studied the picture on the laptop. "If they are in the old hanger, then we may be able to capture them without much effort. Can your drones carry rocket launchers?"

Jai looked at him. "No but the helicopters do. What do you have in mind?"

"Let's fire a missile into the other building. It appears not to be used because the roof has huge holes. That should give them plenty of reasons to consider not shooting their way out."

Jai ordered one of the drone pilots to radio the Army commander and get a gunship on its way. It took about ten minutes before the helicopter was on the scene. Jai picked up the portable radio and instructed the pilot to fire a missile into the building on the right with the holes in the roof. It took only seconds before the huge explosion was seen on the drone's monitors. The building nearly collapsed. The drone moved in closer and captured a picture of several men running from the front door. The large doors opened. A car was trying to get out of the building. The Army helicopter asked over the radio what his orders of engagement were. Jai keyed the talk button.

"Keep the car from leaving. Fire some rounds in front of the car. If it doesn't stop then shoot to disable the engine." The sound of a heavy caliber machine gun was heard over the radio. "Do you have armed troops on board to arrest the people trying to escape?"

"Yes sir, we have six men with automatic weapons."

"If the car stops, land and arrest the men in the car. Dispatch some men to also arrest the ones that are on foot. The drone has them under surveillance; the drone pilot can instruct you where they are." He handed the radio to one of the drone pilots.

The helicopter fired four rounds into the hood of the car and landed a few feet away. The car stopped and four men got out. They had guns but quickly placed them on the ground. Six soldiers jumped down from the helicopter and used plastic ties to handcuff all four men. Three of the soldiers ran toward the building. They had ear pieces and could hear the instructions from the drone pilot. The two men running were behind the building and attempting to escape into a wooded area. A tall wire fence surrounded the airfield. The men escaping could not scale the fence. They turned, dropped their weapons and put their hands in the air. The soldiers used zip ties to handcuff the two and marched them back to the front of the building. Jai and Xia had watched the entire thing on the laptop screen which also recorded the entire takedown.

Jai gave instructions to someone on the phone to move the captured men to the MSS office in Shanghai. He felt the investigation was picking up speed. He was very impressed with the CIA agent's information on how Dr. Wu was moved out of China. He could use people like him.

Jai and Nu boarded a helicopter and returned to Shanghai.

Chapter 10

Shanghai

Susan Daley completed most of the arrangements for returning the bodies of her fallen men. Langley was not happy with what had happened. They had lots of questions, but Susan had few answers. She requested assistance in locating Dr. Wu in North Korea. It would be dangerous, but they had to stop Dr. Wu from making the device operational.

Nu knocked on her door and stuck his head around to see if she would be available. She waved him into her office. "Nu, you solved one part of the puzzle. Has there been any break-through on the questioning of the captured men?"

"No. Jai assigned one of his best men to interrogate them. He thought it best if I was not present. I think they did not want us to witness their techniques."

"Well, that may be best. What would be your best guess as to where they took Dr. Wu.?"

"I'm not familiar with the scientific community of North Korea, but I may have someone that is."

"That's great. Contact them and try to find the most likely places they would conduct physics experiments. Don't give any information about why you are making the inquiry."

"Right, I'm on it." Nu left the room and headed to his cubical. He was concerned that maybe he promised too much to his boss.

***

Jai Chun's phone rang. He picked up the receiver and listened. He rubbed his forehead with his other hand. The news was not good. The men picked up were for-hire thugs and knew nothing about what was happening. They confirmed that two women boarded a plane and flew off in the early morning. That's all they knew. Jai replaced the receiver and sat thinking. He had one person that might help. He could not contact that person until after six o'clock. Until then he would concentrate on finding Dr. Wu's aunt. A knock on his door brought him back in focus.

"Yes come in." A woman came in and gave a shallow bow.

"Sir we have finished our search of Wang's apartment and bookshop. We found nothing that would aid us in locating her. We canvassed the entire area. No one came forward with any information."

"Thank you. You may leave now." The woman nodded and left his office. Jai was distraught that the investigation had hit a dead end. He knew the aunt's well being was important so the North Koreans could put pressure on Dr. Wu.

***

Li Ming went to the bathroom and hung her new PJs on the hook on the bathroom door. She undressed and took a shower. It was a stressful day. The pajamas she bought were nice. The fabric felt like silk but she knew it would be nylon or some synthetic. She put on the pajamas and prepared for bed. She was in the process of hanging up her new clothes when Dauen Kim came to her door and asked if she needed anything.

"Thank you no. But I would like to talk." She opened the door and the two sat across from each other in the comfortable sitting room separating the two bedrooms. "Dauen, have the people that selected you for this assignment told you what this is all about?"

Dauen sat for a few seconds looking puzzled. "No, I was told that a very important scientist was arriving and that I was to assist you in any way. Do you know what we will be working on?" That remark surprised Li Ming. Dauen had no idea what the project entailed.

"Dauen, I have been taken by force from Shanghai and brought here against my will. They want me to work on a device that is far from being functional. In fact, I may not be able to get it to work at all. They have kidnapped my only living relative and are forcing me to work or they will harm her."

Dauen looked shocked. Li Ming knew she had no idea of what had taken place. "Dauen, is there a way you can contact your husband and determine if he is okay?"

"I don't know. We have no phone. The man that is the supervisor of our building has one, but I'm not sure of the number. I could call my sister and have her go by our home and speak to my husband and let me know if he and my children are safe."

Li Ming sat thinking. "Before you call your sister, did the people that contacted you about this assignment make any threats or any promises?" Dauen's face was a blank. No emotions showed. She sat very still and stared at Li Ming.

A loud knock at the door broke the tension. Dauen got up and answered the door. Two men in suits stood in the hall. One spoke to Dauen in Korean and pulled her to the hall. The door slammed shut. Li Ming sat in silence. After a couple of minutes the door opened and Dauen returned to the room. The two men were gone. She had tears on her cheeks and went directly to her bedroom and closed the door. Li Ming knew the rooms were bugged. They did not want Dauen to contact her sister or anyone. She was as much a prisoner as Li Ming.

Li Ming went to her bedroom and turned off the lights. She turned on the light in the bathroom and opened the door a crack to allow a small amount of light into the bedroom. She began to examine the walls, fixtures, lamps and furniture. Within four minutes, she found a hidden camera behind the mirror hanging over a dresser. She thought, *Not good.* She went into the bathroom looking for cameras. She found none. It was the only place in the apartment that was not under observation. She had to tell Dauen what she had found—not now but tomorrow.

Chapter 11

Shanghai

Zhon Wang was concerned that Li Ming did not return to get her backpack. She decided to call Xia and have him check with Li Ming's aunt at her bookshop. Xia answered on the first ring.

Hi sister, what's up?" Xia , for a seventeen year old was very mature and extremely curious.

"Li Ming left her backpack here and hasn't returned. Can you go by her aunt's bookshop and deliver it for me?"

"Sure, I'm just coming up the steps to your room." Xia was very interested in Li Ming's incidents. He was curious and watched all the detective shows on TV. He really wanted to be a detective.

"Oh. Good. I'll meet you with the backpack." She grabbed the backpack and headed to the hallway. Xia was just getting to the top of the stairs. "Hi, thank you so much for doing this. Something is not right. I checked with some of the department people and they said the symposium was cancelled in the afternoon because so many decided not to attend. I asked about Li Ming and they said she got into an argument with a man from North Korea. She left and was seen getting into a car.

Xia studied his sister's face. "I'll go now. There seems to be more going on than we know about. I saw two men being arrested at the bookshop. They looked Korean. Li Ming seemed very concerned and did not want to contact her aunt. With what she told us that happened, I'm thinking she may be in real danger."

"Yes, and you be very careful. There may be people looking for her and you don't want to get caught up in something dangerous."

"OK. I'll call you when I get to the bookshop." Xia left and made his way to the subway station that would take him to the area of the bookshop.

The trip took him about twenty minutes. He slung the backpack over his shoulder and walked to the bookshop. Everything looked normal. There were no police cars and people were walking along and entering shops. He walked slowly past the bookshop. There was a sign on the door stating the bookshop was closed. He did not notice a dark van parked down the street.

Xia decided to go up the stairs to the apartment above the shop. He knocked on the door but no one answered. He turned and was coming down the steps when two men blocked his way.

One of the men came up to Xia and asked his name and what was his business with the owner of the bookshop. The man had a Korean accent. "I'm delivering something to her." He didn't want to say much more.

"What are you delivering? Xia decided not to reveal he had Li Ming's backpack. "I came to pay for a book. I didn't have money when I was here. She told me to take the book and bring the money later. I came today to pay her."

The men looked at him and nodded. "Okay, you can go. She will not be back for a few days." They moved out of Xia's way so he could exit to the street. He saw the alley across the street where he and Li Ming had waited. He decided to go down the alley and return to see what the men did.

He walked down the alley for a short way and stopped. He turned and saw the men get into a dark van parked in front of the shop. He heard a noise behind him and a hand grabbed his arm. He was startled. The man identified himself as with the police. He didn't show any ID or have a badge. The man was Chinese.

"Come with me" said the man. They went down the alley away from the bookshop. Another man and a woman joined them and no one spoke. They reached the end of the alley. A dark colored SUV was parked around the corner. The woman opened the rear door and motioned for Xia to get in. The two men got in the front and the woman got in beside Xia.

The woman took out a small recording device. "What is your name?"

"I am Xia Wang. Am I in some sort of trouble?"

"No we saw you go to the apartment above the shop and those

men stopping you. We are investigating the disappearance of the shop owner. Do you know anything about where she could be?"

Xia sat very still. He looked at the woman's face. She seemed at ease and was not trying to intimidate. "I don't know the shop owner. I was here to deliver this backpack. It belongs to Dr. Wu, I met her yesterday. She left it at my sister's dorm room at Fudan University."

One of the men turned and nodded at the woman. "Xia, we are very concerned about Dr. Wu Li Ming, the lady you met yesterday. She is in danger and may have been taken away by some very bad people. Do you mind if I look inside the backpack? It may give us a clue as to where she may have been taken."

Xia handed the backpack to the woman. She opened and examined its contents. There were several items of clothing, a make-up mirror and a large scientific calculator. There were no notes or anything that could identify who the backpack belonged to.

Xia looked on as the woman put all the items back inside the backpack. "I'm going to keep this and will give it to Li Ming when we find her."

"Okay. I did notice one thing, her laptop and notebook are missing. She had them when she was in my sister's room. She may have taken them to the symposium. She didn't return to my sister's room after the symposium."

"Can you call your sister and find out if she left the laptop and notebook in the dorm room?"

"Sure." Xia pulled the iPhone from his jeans and entered in the number for Zhon. "Sis, did Li Ming leave her laptop and notebook in your room?" He listened for a few seconds. "Okay, thanks. I'll be going home from the bookshop and see you tomorrow." He listened and pressed the end call button. "She took the laptop and notebook with her to the symposium."

"Thank you Xia. If you think of anything else, here is a number you can call." She gave him a card with the number. The man in the passenger's seat got out and opened the door to let Xia out.

"Oh, I remember a man on a motorcycle coming by while Li Ming and I watched from this alley. He wore a red helmet with a large yellow lightning bolt. I had never seen one like it." Xia turned to leave. The man that had opened his door tapped him on the shoulder.

"Do you think you could identify the man?"

"No sir, his helmet had a darken visor. I did not see his face."

"Okay, thanks. You may go."

Xia walked back up the alley. He was very concerned about Li Ming and her aunt. They must be very important having so much happen to them and all these people looking for them.

He began his walk home. He had walked about six blocks when he heard a motorcycle. The machine passed him. The driver was wearing a red helmet with a bright yellow lightning bolt. He saw the bike slow and go into a parking area in front of a tall apartment building. Xia made note of the bikes license plate number and the address of the building.

He took out his phone and called the number on the card. The woman answered. He told her where he was and that he may have found the man on the motorcycle. The woman told Xia to stay out of sight that they would be there in five minutes.

***

A dark SUV cruised down the street. It stopped just past the apartment building. Two men got out and walked back to the building. They were examining the bike. One took out his phone and took a picture. He then spoke into his phone and the woman got out and walked to meet them.

Xia was well concealed behind a tall wall that surrounded a courtyard. The gate was open and he stood just inside and watched the three people who said they were with the police. They were talking with each other when two more SUV's arrived and four men from each of the cars got out and joined the three. They spoke for a few minutes and then two of the men went down an alley to the back of the apartment building. Two of the men took up positions at the base of the fire escape. The others started into the building when shots rang out.

One of the men fell. Xia saw the man crawl to the side of the building. It was apparent he was wounded. The woman and two of the men pulled guns and stormed into the front door. More shots rang out. The two men at the base of the fire escape were shooting at someone on the fire escape ladder. Several more shots were fired. Xia could not determine who was doing the shooting. He stayed behind the wall.

The woman came out the front door and waved at one of the men crouched down near the front door. They immediately ran into the building. For several minutes there was no more gun fire. Xia eased his head around the gate to get a better view. He saw three of the men come out of the door with two men in handcuffs. They made them sit down on the pavement. One of the SUV men was talking on his phone.

The woman came out helping an older woman walk towards one of the SUVs. A large van came down the street. It had POLICE written on the side. It stopped in front of the apartment building. Xia couldn't see what was happening. Then the rear doors to the van were opened by one of the men. Two of the men had each man with cuffs by the arms and made them get into the back of the police van. One of the men followed the handcuffed men into the van. The doors were shut and the van left.

The woman assisted the older woman to get into the back of their SUV. She closed the door and looked up and down the street. There were several people standing in their doorways observing what was going on. She looked toward Xia and motioned for him to come to her.

"Xia, I want to thank you for your help finding some of the bad guys. She smiled. You are a good detective. The woman is Dr. Wu's aunt. Mrs. Wang"

Xia could feel his face flush with embarrassment. "My name is Wang also."

The police woman spoke with several of the men. She was carrying a strange looking phone. One of the men walked over to the motorcycle and placed a plastic tie through the spokes and the front fork of the bike. The man stayed with the bike and the others got in their cars and left with the older woman.

Xia had a smile on his face and a spring in his step as he walked home.

Chapter 12

Somewhere in North Korea

Li Ming spent a restless night. She had not seen Dauen since she went to her room the night before. She got dressed into one of the outfits they had purchased. It was drab but comfortable. She filled the kettle and put it on the burner. The dishes were old but clean. The tea was in a tin on the counter and she put two scoops in the metal strainer and placed it in the pot. Within a few minutes the aroma was filling the small kitchen.

The door opened and Dauen came out. She was dressed and kept her eyes down. She went to the tea pot and poured a cup of hot tea. Nothing was said. She turned to Li Ming and held her finger over her mouth indicating not to speak.

Li Ming went to the table and got a pen and paper. She drew a camera and microphones. She motioned for Dauen to follow her into the bathroom. She closed the door. In a whispered voice she told Dauen what she had discovered. "This is the only place not being observed. We should speak in normal tones and only about work. Don't talk about your family or anyone you know." Dauen nodded her understanding.

They went back into the small sitting room and drank tea. "Dauen, I would like to go to the place we will work. How do we get there?"

"There will be a car here at seven thirty to take us to the lab. I was told it's only a short ride away. Li Ming smiled and sipped her tea.

So Dauen had not been to the lab. "We have fifteen minutes before the car is here. Do we wait for them someplace or will they come and fetch us?"

"They will come to the door and escort us to the car." Dauen looked down at the table. She was still unsure about her role. She still shook at thinking about the men that came to their door the past evening. She picked up her tea cup and went to the sink. She ran water into the cup and placed it in the sink. A knock at the door broke the silence. "That will be our ride to work."

Li Ming placed her cup in the sink and waited until Dauen opened the door to one man standing in the hall. He spoke briefly to Dauen in Korean and stepped back. Dauen turned to Li Ming. "He says for us to follow him to the car now."

The three walked down a flight of stairs. Another man stood beside a Honda and opened the back door when he saw them emerge from the apartment building. He motioned for Li Ming and Dauen to get in the back. They drove past a large hotel and through a residential area for several minutes. The car eventually turned onto a wide avenue. The buildings appeared to be office buildings. It was hard for her to determine.

The car slowed and turned into a drive that led to an underground garage. The car pulled up to two men in uniform. They opened the doors to the car. One of the soldiers spoke to the driver. He responded with a few words. The other man in the passenger's seat turned and spoke to Dauen. She nodded and got out of the car. She told Li Ming to follow her. They entered a stair well and went up several flights of stairs.

A man in front of them pushed open a door to a brightly lit hallway. He remained at the door. A man in a white lab coat came and bowed to Li Ming. He spoke in Mandarin. "I am Dr. Siu. Welcome to our laboratory. Dr. Wu your work is well known. Please follow me" He escorted Dauen and Li Ming into a large lab with five people in lab coats working at various machines and computers.

They entered a conference room that was along the interior wall of the lab. There was a long table with a man and a woman seated. The woman did not wear a lab coat. The man was middle age and sported a mustache and goatee. He rose as they came into the room. Their escort bowed to the group and closed the door as he left.

"I am Chui Kwang and this is Rhee Sung-min. We will be working with you on this project." He motioned for all to sit down. Dauen kept her eyes down and said nothing.

"Exactly what is this project you are working on?" said Li Ming.

Kwang smiled and turned to the woman. She did not smile and was very serious looking. "I think you know what we are working on and why you are here. We can do this several ways. You can cooperate or we will make a phone call to have your aunt persuade you to cooperate. Now which is it going to be?", said Sung-min. She stared directly into Li Ming's eyes.

"I will try to assist you. I don't have much hope in making the device function. It was not operational in our lab at Cal Tech. We had not been successful in making any thing transfer in whole. Each sample was modified or destroyed in the attempt."

"That is not what we were told. In fact we know you succeeded in moving a rather large object several times. Dr. March is crowing about your success."

Li Ming sat with a blank stare at the man. The woman removed a picture from a folder on the table. "This is a picture taken only this morning of your aunt. If you value her life you will do as we ask. Do you understand?"

Li Ming said nothing. Dauen sat very still. It was obvious this was the first time she knew the circumstances in which Li Ming was brought to North Korea.

Kwang stood and went to a laptop computer set up on a countertop that went down one wall of the room. He entered some information. The screen lit up. Li Ming recognized the information from her laptop. They must have retrieved it from the safe house. "You will recognize the diagrams. We need to concentrate on the power supply. We can't seem to get a stable ion flow. This is your first assignment. Get a steady flow of ions and then we will know if the device can be functional." He turned to Li Ming. "Please follow me to the lab."

They left the conference room and entered a huge lab with many work benches and instruments. Li Ming saw her device on a table near the back of the room. Two people in lab coats were working on the device.

Li Ming saw a makeshift power supply. That explained why they were concentrating on the power supply. The one they had built from her notes did not work properly. That was a break. It would take a long time to reconstruct the power supply to the specifications necessary to active the device. Even then without the special component that she had left in her backpack, they were never going to get the device to work properly.

Chapter 13

The Physics lab in North Korea

Li Ming watched as a lab technician fiddled with the power supply. Kwang motioned for her to step closer. She moved to the bench the power supply occupied.

"Dr. Wu, what do you think is the problem?" He focused on the word think.

"Without detailed readings of the various components I cannot venture a guess." She saw they had several instruments attached, but none that gave the output readings.

"I will leave you to direct these technicians in resolving the issues with the power supply." He turned and left the room. Dauen stood to one side without speaking.

Li Ming asked one of the technicians to connect an oscilloscope to the output transformer. The technician shook his head and said something to Dauen in Korean. "He does not speak Mandarin" said Dauen.

"Oh fine. This is going to be a long session." Li Ming shook her head. "You translate for me. Tell him to connect the scope."

Dauen explained to the technician what Dr. Wu wanted. He nodded and spoke to the other technician, who went to a shelf to get the scope and attach it to the power supply. The screen lit up and showed a wide band of activity. Li Ming adjusted the amplitude and the width. She noted that the amplitude was only a fraction of what it should be. There were many components that could cause this. One was the use of the wrong size coupling capacitors. She decided to go slow on the examination, but do a complete analysis. The technicians would understand the caution and appreciate the thoroughness. Two hours went by and the pattern on the scope had not changed. Several components had been replaced but did not fix the problem.

Dauen spoke to the technicians. They smiled and bowed to Li Ming. "What did you say to them?" asked Li Ming.

"I asked them if we could take a break and have some chai." Li

Ming laughed and returned the bow to the technicians. They spoke to Dauen and pointed to a door across the lab. "They said there is a break room across the hall. We have to get permission to leave the lab."

One of the lab technicians spoke to the guard at the door. He spoke into his radio and nodded to the technician. The four walked to the door and it was immediately opened by someone in the hall who evidently had a view of the interior of the lab.

The break room was small but had a table that could seat six. They each poured a cup of tea. There were some pastries on a plate. Dauen took the entire plate and sat it in front of the group. They sipped their tea and nibbled on the pastries. No one spoke.

Li Ming saw a camera in each corner of the room. They were constantly being monitored. No different than her lab in California. Dauen had begun to speak to the younger of the two lab techs. She had asked their names. The older one spoke. "Jung" He pointed at the younger man and said, "Jae" They all smiled.

A guard came in and told Dauen it was time to return to the lab. They put their tea cups into the bin on the counter and returned to the lab. The scope was still displaying the wave forms which remained only a fraction of what they should be.

Li Ming saw her note book on the bench next to a computer terminal. She smiled when she realized it was in English. None of these people would be able to interpret the notes. On the screen was text in Korean. "Dauen, is this a translation of my notes?"

Dauen looked at the screen. "Yes. I don't read English, but it appears to be a translation of technical notes."

"Okay, we may have discovered why the power supply isn't working. The measuring scales are different. I used English measurements and they are translating them as metric. Every component in the power supply is under or over sized. We must rebuild the power supply using the correct size components."

Li Ming had no more than finished telling Dauen her finding when the lab door burst open and Kang and Sung-min came through. Kwang came up to the group and examined the notebook and read several screens of data on the computer. "She is right; some idiot had taken all the English component sizes as metric." Sung-min looked at the lab techs with distain.

"Who translated these notes?" asked Kang.

Jung spoke. There was silence. Sung-min turned and left the room. Kwang picked up the note book and left also.

"What was that all about?" asked Li Ming.

"They confirmed what you said. The measurements are in metric not English. They are very upset. A full month wasted on constructing the power supply."

Li Ming had to suppress a smile. She knew they were being monitored. This was good news. It would take her at least three weeks to build the power supply.

***

Susan Daley was pleased with the extraction of Li Ming's aunt. She was now in a safe place. The satellite phone was also in her possession. She and Nu had a plan. If it rang, they would answer it and pretend to be one of the thugs the MSS had locked up. It was highly unlikely that the controllers would recognize the hired thug's voice. They had briefed the aunt on their plan. The North Koreans would think Li Ming's aunt was still under their control.

Jai Chun was happy with the results of working with Susan. He felt his people were contributing to the investigation. He had two Korean speaking agents with two of Susan's agents.

***

Seok Dong-Suk was pleased he had successfully captured Dr. Wu. It would be only a matter of time before they had the device working and North Korea would take its rightful place on the world stage. The Chairman was pleased.

The lab was secure and only fully vetted people knew of its existence. His operative, Sung-min, was one of his best. She would make sure Dr. Wu cooperated.

The last report from Sung-min was disappointing, but she was confident this would be corrected within a month. The military was ordered to stay out of the game for the time being. He knew if they got involved, things could get out of hand concerning the well being of Dr. Wu. That was not an option at the moment.

Chapter 14

Cal Tech

Dr. March hung up his phone. He was very disturbed. His conversation with Susan Daley was unsettling. He had been told by the Chancellor to expect a call from the CIA operative. She had been cleared for full disclosure.

She told him Li Ming was in danger and they suspected the North Koreans. The CIA had Li Ming in a safe house for the time being. She also confirmed that it was the North Koreans that stole the teleportation device from Li Ming's lab.

Dr. March confirmed to Ms Daley that the last experiment was successful and explained how Li Ming had etched a Lotus leaf on the solid steel test object. It had been successfully moved to the next room and returned. The etching was intact and the object was not altered in any way. No one else knew about the test. It had been done late at night and was the day before the device was stolen. He wondered how did the North Koreans know of the project, much less that it had been successful?

He called his secretary to assemble the entire team in the conference room in one hour.

Dr. March was very concerned about the well being of Li Ming. She had become like a daughter he never had. He thought she was the most brilliant physicist he had ever known and worked hard to keep up with her drive to make the transporter work. That was what she called the device. She had become a fan of Star trek.

Dr. March opened up a Word document on his computer and typed a series of questions for his team. Although he was unsure of the impact of what Ms Daley had told him, he was sure of the significance of the experiments Li Ming had been conducting. He looked at the antique clock on his desk. It was time to go.

The room was full of his team. The chatter stopped as he took his place at the head of the table. "Team, I have some very disturbing news. It appears that we know the North Koreans are the ones who stole our device. I have just been told that Dr. Wu is in danger of being kidnapped by the North Koreans." He looked around the room at each face for reactions. They all looked stunned. "However there are people protecting her." He looked down at the hand-out his secretary had placed before each team member.

"You each have a hand-out with some questions. It is essential that we are all in agreement as to the actions we need to take. We do not have any idea why the device was taken and of what use it would be to the North Koreans. Having said that, let's go down the list of questions one by one. First question, do we reconstruct the device?"

They all looked at one another. Dr. Fazler the senior scientist raised his hand. "Dr. Fazler?" said Dr. March.

"Dr. March, team, I think the machine should be rebuilt. We were very close to success when the machine was stolen. We have been through all the trials and failures. We know how to build the machine without those flaws. I suggest we rebuild." Dr. Fazler sat down. There was complete silence. All were looking at Dr. March.

"Thank you Dr. Fazler. Before we examine your proposal, I would like to address some of the obvious questions dealing with building some of the unique components and how long this would take. The next item is the ion generator. As you know this was a challenge and we had many failures. Can we rebuild that component without the same flaws?" asked Dr. March. "Dr. Vaden you were the leader on that team. What do you say about rebuilding the ion generator?"

Dr. Vaden took his time. He looked at the table for several seconds. "I agree we had difficulty building a working model. I feel we overcame the flaws and the final version can be rebuilt within two weeks." Several of his team nodded in agreement.

"Thank you Dr. Vaden. Are there any comments?" There were no hands raised. "Okay, next item is the focus coil component. Can we rebuild this component without going back to the drawing board?" One of the two female scientists raised her hand.

"Sir, we already have a working coil. We were concerned about the heat ratio and built a backup just in case. It is ready." Gloria Stein smiled at her companions.

"Wonderful Gloria, that will save us a lot of time. The next item is a big one. Can we rebuild the oscillator? This took a year to get working. Can it be rebuilt with all the precision of the stolen one?" Dr. March looked around the table. The faces were ones of concern. "People, we must consider the possibility that we may not be able to rebuild certain components to the same precision. But if we are going to rebuild we must have an accurate time line."

A very young man raised his hand. He was in charge of managing all data storage and maintaining all the computers. "Sir, we have all the final data on the oscillator. We should be able to download it to the lab computers and the techies can begin as soon as you give the word. The data contains all the flaws and points out the corrections. It should be a piece of cake to rebuild the final version with the same precision."

"Mr. Johnson, building this complex device is not a piece of cake. But if you are right I'll bake you the best cake you ever had." The room burst into nervous laughter. It was the tension breaker needed.

Dr. March checked the other questions. "As you can see on your hand-out, the remaining components are critical, but manageable with off the shelf parts. If there is no objection, I would like a vote on re-building the teleport."

Every one raised his hand. The room burst into conversations and slaps on the back. They were all together as a team. The only person missing was Li Ming. No one knew she had the missing component and it could not be replicated without her. She had put the entire design and software in her hidden safe in her office. A picture of Ronald Reagan hung over the safe.

The next day, the lab team was hard at work. Dr. March stayed out of their way. His phone rang. It was Susan Daley from Shanghai.

"Yes Ms Daley, tell me all is okay." He listened and bolted upright when she told him Li Ming had been kidnapped and most likely was already in North Korea. Li Ming's aunt was also missing and assumed to have been kidnapped also, but she said she did not think they had taken her to North Korea. Four of her officers had been killed.

"This is awful. I am so sorry for your loss. What can I do?"

"Dr. March, rebuild that machine and get it working ASAP. We have a theory about what the North Koreans plan on using it for, but

I'm not at liberty to say. I will keep you informed on any change in the situation" said Susan Daley.

Dr. March said bye and hung up his phone. This was now personal. They had Li Ming and were using her aunt as leverage to get cooperation. He had to motivate his people to get the machine rebuilt as soon as possible. Something dire was in the works and must involve using the device for something that is top secret.

He decided to name the project *The Lotus Project*.

Chapter 15

Shanghai

Susan Daley began making plans. She knew that Li Ming was not being harmed. They needed her to make the device work. She needed a new commander for Shanghai. John Peterson was killed at the safe house along with the others. She decided to make Nu Lee acting commander in charge of the Shanghai office. Officially there was no office, but everyone knew there were three, Beijing, Hong Kong and Shanghai.

Nu knocked on her door. "Come in Nu. Have you heard from your source on the most likely location they would test the device?"

"Yes. The most likely is a small city south of Pyongyang. It is the center of their nuclear program. They have all the equipment necessary to test any kind of electronic device. There is an elite military group guarding the facilities. My source says no one has ever been able to breach the security."

"Hum, that doesn't sound good. I am trying to get someone from the NSA to check on any chatter that may be helpful, but so far nothing."

"Madam Daley, I may have an idea."

Please call me Susan. Okay let's hear it."

"When the North Koreans check in with the group that are holding Dr. Wu's aunt, we get the NSA to triangulate the call. That will at least tell us where they are located. Then we can come up with a strategy to extract Dr. Wu." Susan sat and listened carefully.

"Nu, I'll get right on it. It's been two days and no call has come through. I hope the thugs were not supposed to initiate the call."

Nu shook his head. "From my observation of the quality of their team, I'd say the call will be initiated from North Korea. I have another concern. There must still be a mole in Cal Tech that was reporting on Dr. Wu's project to the North Koreas. I sent a message to our office in Pasadena. I haven't heard back"

"Good work Nu. I had forgotten about how the North Koreans

knew about the work of Dr. Wu. When you get a report, let me know."

Nu Lee left Susan Daley's office and returned to his cubical. She had told him he could use John Peterson's office, but he felt it was too soon to do so. The other staff didn't know him that well and may feel hostile to a newbie coming in and taking over. He needed a loyal team to pursue this case.

Susan placed a call to her NSA contact in Washington. One of her technicians had pulled the sat phone's number and data address. Susan gave her contact the information and explained what she wanted. The contact assured her if a call was made to that phone they would know within ten feet of where it originated.

Susan had a large screen TV in her office and had connected a laptop. A detailed map of North Korea was displayed. When the NSA gave her the coordinates, she would know where Li Ming was being held. Getting her back would be a whole lot more complicated.

Los Angeles

William Braun arrived at LAX early in the morning from Shanghai. He had gotten little sleep. He spotted one of his men waiting at the exit door to the customs hall. He cleared customs and joined his man.

Joseph Bell was a seasoned veteran of the FBI. His specialty was creating a network of informants throughout southern California. William was on a tight schedule. The bosses in Washington wanted a closure to the Cal Tech case. All the Intel agencies had heard of the loss of the agents in Shanghai.

"Joe, any chatter about the theft at Cal Tech?"

"No sir. No one knows anything. It is as if these guys flew in one day and out the next with the stolen items.

"There must be a mole in the lab at Cal Tech. That place is as tight as a drum and most of the staff is from Area 51. My bet is on someone who is not on the team but has access to what is happening in the labs. They could be part of the cleaning staff, a girl friend, a secretary or one of the guards. I've been thinking that it is someone who has an ax to grind. I've had some of our group doing deep background checks on anyone who is authorized to enter the lab building. So far, there are over one hundred individuals that have some business in the building. We may have a suspect list by late today."

"Good work Joe. I'm not going to go into the office today. I'm bushed and have to get some sleep. Call me if something breaks."

"Yes sir." Joe returned to the FBI office in downtown Pasadena. He checked into the small room where he had several of the staff doing extended background checks on anyone that had access to the lab building. They were especially looking for anyone who had any social media personas that advocated against the government. So far nothing had turned up.

The day had gone by slowly. It was 6 p.m. and .Joe was in the process of typing his daily report when one of the agents doing the background checks knocked on his door. "Sir, I may have something. One of the secretaries working for a lab technician has been posting stuff about the treatment of illegal aliens. She also travels to anti government rallies and participates in something named CFER Citizens For Equal Rights. She is single and has worked at the lab for the past two years. Prior to that she was a student at Berkley. I suggest we put a tail on her for a few days." The agent handed over the folder with all the details.

Joe read the entire folder of documents while the agent waited. On the surface, the secretary appeared to be just a protester. "Okay, put a 24/7 tail on her and let's see what she may be up to." The agent nodded and left the office.

The agents assigned to tail Mary Rodriguez set up a schedule and plan for surveillance. There were four teams of two.

The second day of the surveillance, an agent noted she left the lab building at noon and drove to a park on the north side of Pasadena. She exited her car and walked to a play area. Several mothers were watching their kids play on the rides.

Mary took a seat on a bench. She opened a bag and took out a sandwich and a bottle of water. She took her time eating. A woman walking a dog came down the path and took a seat next to Mary. They spoke to each other but the agents didn't see anything pass between the two women.

The woman with the dog got up and continued on down the path. Mary folded the paper wrappers and deposited them in a rubbish bin beside the path. She walked back to her car and drove away. One of the agents followed her as the other agent continued to watch the rubbish bin.

A man dressed in denim work clothes took the lid off the rubbish bin and removed the folded paper bag and wrappers. The agent quickly approached the man and arrested him. He placed the folded bag and wrappers into an evidence bag. The man protested that he had done nothing wrong. The agent radioed he had apprehended someone of interest and to send backup.

The evidence bag was opened by a lab technician in the forensics lab at the FBI office in L.A. The bag was examined but contained nothing of interest. The sandwich wrappers contain a typed note. The note read: Work has begun to rebuild the device. Parts have been ordered.

Joseph Bell immediately phoned his boss William Braun. "Sir we think we have caught our mole. She is a secretary to one of the lab technicians. She used a dead drop at a park. The information she dropped tells someone that a device is being rebuilt and parts have been ordered."

Joe listened for a few seconds. "Yes sir, we have eyes on her and will bring her in within the next hour." Joseph punched off the call and punched another number into his iPhone.

"Bring Mary Rodriguez in for questioning." Joe pressed the end button. He was pleased with the team. It remained to be seen if they can connect Mary Rodriguez to the North Koreans.

Los Angeles FBI Offices

William Braun drove into the parking garage below the offices of the FBI in L.A. The two suspects had been transported there from Pasadena.

William watched from a darken room. The woman was adamant she had done nothing and deserved to be released.

The man was being interviewed in an adjacent room. He said nothing.

One of the FBI's best profilers was brought in to the interrogation room. She sat and said nothing while an agent was asking Mary questions. Most of the questions were about her job, her education, her hobbies and mundane things. Nothing was asked about the drop. She had not been told that she had been observed dropping the information in the rubbish bin.

William pressed a button and a light blinked on the wall behind Mary. It was the signal to begin the real questioning. The profiler opened a folder and asked Mary if she was a member of a protest group. Mary looked at her for a long time.

"Yes, I am a member of the Citizens for Equal Rights."

"What does this organization do exactly?" asked the profiler.

"We demonstrate for those who we feel are not being given equal rights under the law. There are many people being held illegally and without proper representation. Is that what his is all about?"

The profiler sat back and did not respond to Mary's question. The agent opened the folder and flipped several pages. "Ms. Rodriguez, who do you know in that organization?" Mary looked questionably at the agent.

"I know several members. I've never met them personally, but I have talked and texted them."

"So, you actually don't know the leaders of the organization and have met only members during a rally."

"Yes."

The profiler leaned forward. "Mary when did you join the group?"

"I joined about three years ago. A man came to my dorm at Berkley and spoke to several of us. He explained how people were being held without due process of law and that would we help them by protesting."

The profiler studied a document. "Mary, were you asked to get specific information for the group."

Mary just stared at the table. "Yes, I was told that some of the work being done in the labs at Cal Tech was illegal and they needed to know what type of work was being done in the lab where I worked. We would expose the illegal work."

The agent asked, "Mary how did you deliver this information to this organization?

"I was told that certain government agents were watching members of the organization and to put the report in a rubbish bin in Staunton Park to be safe. I couldn't get much information on what was happening in the lab. Mostly my boss would tell me things and to order parts needed in the construction of some device."

"Mary, did you ever meet anyone you were to pass this information to?

"No, I received a phone call once. They asked for me to photograph the device being built. Of course I couldn't because I was not allowed into the lab itself" said Mary.

"Did you know the person that phoned you?" asked the agent.

"No, I didn't know the person. They had a strange accent and their English was bad."

"Did you phone anyone the information?"

"No, I was told to type a report every two weeks and put the paper in the rubbish bin at the park. Mostly the report was one or two lines. Just the status of what was happening in the lab."

The profiler and the agent exchange looks. The light behind Mary blinked. The agent and the profiler got up. "We will be back in a moment. Would you like anything to drink?" asked the profiler.

"No thank your" said Mary.

The two left the interrogation room and entered the observation room. William Braun had watched the entire processes. "Either she is a good liar or is very gullible. I don't think she realizes that she is a member of a fake organization. Her information only told the North Koreans that something was being built and that most of the people working on the project were from Area 51. She basically reported on the progress of the construction and testing. She had no idea what the machine was to do and for that matter, we don't either." William was not happy.

The profiler nodded she was in agreement with William. "I will explain what she has done and that she may be detained." She turned and went back to the interrogation room.

William saw Mary begin to cry. She was taken advantage of by some very clever North Korean agents. He would phone this information to Susan Daley in Shanghai.

Chapter 16

Pasadena

Susan Daley worked all night. She was the only one in the office. Her phone rang and was surprised anyone would be up at this hour. "Yes, this is Susan." She listened and giggled. "William, you know we never sleep. What's the good news?"

"Susan, we have uncovered our mole. She is the secretary to one of the lab technicians. She had no clue she was involved with the North Koreans and that she was leaking classified information. She thought she was helping some fake group get evidence of illegal government use of the Cal Tech Labs." Susan made a frown.

"William, are you sure she did not know about the North Koreans?"

"Yes, she had no idea what the device was built for and had never seen it. They had asked her to photo the item, but she was not allowed in the lab itself. So we closed this part of the case but without really accomplishing anything. I'm not sure if she will be prosecuted."

"Thanks for the update William. We did extract Dr. Wu's aunt. The kidnappers were hired from a local North Korean crime family. They know nothing about why they were holding Dr. Wu's aunt."

"Well, good hunting and again I'm sorry for your loss." William put the phone down and thought about how close he came to being in that safe house. If his boss had not ordered him to return that day, he may be dead. William was not a believer of fate, but he didn't believe in luck either.

North Korea Lab

Dauen cried most of the night. She was sad and concerned about her husband and children. Li Ming tossed and turned most of the night. Her body ached and she had a headache. She knew Dauen now realized how desperate the North Koreans were to get the device to work.

The lab technicians arrived at 0700 each morning. As a group, they were young and very smart. They were almost finished with diagramming the device and all of its components. It would not be long before they realized there was a vital piece of software missing.

Dauen and Li Ming worked at a bench next to the one containing the device. The power supply was about half finished.

Li Ming observed the group next to her struggle to interpret some of the software. There were large blank boxes on the screen of the computer used to compose the software diagram. The custom made IC's (integrated circuits) would be almost impossible to diagram without destroying them.

Jung and Jae Kwang came into the lab. They stood behind Li Ming and observed for several minutes. Kwang stepped forward. "Dr. Wu, we would like to speak to you. Please follow us to the conference room. Dauen will not be needed." Dauen lowered her eyes and stood very still. Li Ming nodded to Dauen and followed Kwang and Jung out of the lab.

Kwang closed the door and motioned for all to sit. "Dr. Wu, we would like for you to bring us up-to-date on the progress you are making on the power supply."

Li Ming looked him in the eye. "We are about half way done. The focus coil has to be completely rebuilt. The first one was defective. I have drawn detail specs for the machine shop to make the mechanical parts. Dauen has ordered the correct gauge of wire to complete the coil. If the machine shop completes their part by the end of the week, then I estimate no more than another week to apply the windings to the coil and test."

Jung sat and stared at Li Ming. She leaned forward, "You will speed up the process. We are behind almost a month."

Li Ming leaned forward and looked into Jung's eyes as if to challenge her. "There is no way to speed up the process. We are working twelve hours a day. Mistakes may be made that would damage the power supply if we are not very careful with the coil. I would like to speak to my aunt."

Kwang looked at Jung and she nodded. He reached into a drawer and took out a satellite phone. He pressed a key. "This is Kwang, put the woman on the phone." Kwang waited for a few seconds. He heard the old woman's sleepy voice answer in mandarin. He handed the phone to Li Ming. "Aunt, are you okay. Have they harmed you?" She heard her aunt's voice and was relieved she appeared unharmed.

"Li Ming, they will not allow me to order more books. Your favorite has been misplaced. You know how you liked to read it daily." said her aunt. Li Ming didn't say anything back. She knew someone may be listening in on the conversation. Her aunt was trying to tell her something but what?

Kwang reached for the phone. "Aunt I have to go now. We will talk again soon." She handed the phone back to Kwang.

"Keep her safe and do not harm her in any way", said Kwang He pressed the end key and placed the phone back in the drawer.

Somewhere in Maryland

It had been two weeks since the CIA request had come in to monitor a satellite phone address.

An alarm went off. The computer showed several rows of information. The man sitting at the console pressed some keys on his keyboard. He smiled and spoke to his boss who had heard the alarm and came to stand behind him. "Gotcha. We know where they're transmitting from."

His boss pointed at the big overhead screen with a map of North Korea. "Put it on the map." A large circle and a small x within the circle displayed on the screen. "I want to know everything about that location down to who collects the rubbish." He walked back to his corner office and picked up the phone. It was 7:10 a.m. in Shanghai. The phone rang twice. A very sleepy voice answered.

"Susan, sorry to wake you but I will be sending you a burst in about ten minutes with all the information on where that satellite phone is located."

Shanghai

Susan sat straight up in bed. "When did the call come through?" She looked at the clock. "Thanks, I owe you one." She got out of bed and got dressed. Her apartment was in the same building as the office. It was a one minute walk to work. Dr. Wu's aunt also stayed in the building in a special section. It was built to be impregnable.

Susan sat down at her desk and picked up the phone. "This is Susan, I understand you received a call this morning." She listened to the full report from the agent staying with the aunt. "Did she read the script you had prepared?" She heard the agent confirm that the script was read. "Great. Send me the recording." She hung up. It was coming up on 7:45 a.m. and the office would be busy in fifteen minutes.

Susan saw the data burst from the NSA and copied it to the decrypt folder. In less than thirty seconds, the detailed report on the coordinates of the phone call appeared. She transferred them to the map app that would show the location on the big screen.

She saw the call recording file appear on her computer's desktop. She opened the audio file and heard the entire conversation. There was not much, the entire thing was only forty seconds in duration. She heard the aunt read their prepared script and then Kwang's voice telling the thugs to treat her well.

Susan looked up at the map. The circle and x were exactly where Nu's contact predicted. Susan knew this was going to require some decisions at the highest levels. The US had just cause to do whatever was necessary to get Dr. Wu back. How much info would they share with the Chinese? She would have to fight that battle first.

Chapter 17

Pasadena, California

William Braun knew the FBI would be discharged from the case as soon as the arrest warrant was executed for the secretary. It was out of his hands. He wanted to help Susan's group but that was an entirely different agency with their own rules. It was afternoon in Washington so he phoned his boss. He thought he may as well get this over and settled.

His boss answered the phone on the second ring. "Boss this is William. We have our mole and it appears she is totally in the dark." He listened for his boss' reply. He was shocked when his boss told him that the FBI was not through with the incident at Cal Tech.

"Yes sir, I will have my team waiting for your call." William broke the connection and sat staring at a picture of Bill Clinton. What possible interest could the FBI have in this case? It was a dead end. The woman was duped and that was it. She really had no idea what was happening. She actually thought she was a member of a do-gooder group who were trying to find dirt on the government.

William pressed a button on his phone. His secretary answered. "Marge, have the entire team here for a special meeting at 7pm." She acknowledged. He hung up.

Washington, D.C.

The deputy director of the FBI called a meeting with the Secretary of Defense, the director of the CIA, the director of the NSA and the Secretary of State. They met in the Pentagon..

The meeting began with the deputy director bringing all up-to-date. They knew where Dr. Wu was being held. The CIA had eyes on the location and knew where Li Ming's accommodations were located. They had attempted to give a coded message to Dr. Wu but were not sure if she understood. There was no way to tell.

The CIA director said his asset reported the lab in North Korea was like a fort and would be almost impossible to penetrate. The good news was that the accommodations for Dr. Wu offered an opportunity for a small team to get in and out without too much interference.

The Secretary of Defense asked if there was any chance of getting the device back. The CIA director said the chance of extracting the device was less than ten percent.

The NSA director offered that it may not be necessary to extract the device if they moved within the next forty five days. Without Dr. Wu the device will not work. The North Koreans know that. It may be that Dr. Wu may complete the preliminary repairs within that time frame. Every day she works on the device means our chance of successfully stopping the device from being operational lowers.

The Secretary of State asked the NSA director how they were so certain that the North Koreans could not simply continue to experiment with the device even if Dr. Wu was extracted.

He answered that Dr. March of Cal Tech has assured him that the North Koreans could spend years on the device and never get it to work.

"The question on the table is can we successfully pull off an extraction", asked the Secretary of State.

The group was silent. The Director of the CIA told the group he could assure all that if they attempted an extraction his people could assist on location.

The Secretary of Defense said that he would have to confer with his people before he could commit US forces to attempt such a bold extraction. He said. "This is not Saddam Hussein; this is a battle ship with an unstable rudder." He would have an answer within twenty four hours.

The meeting broke up at 9PM. The deputy director of the FBI made a call to William Braun. "William, be prepared to travel. You are going to be my representative if an extraction team is assembled."

William smiled and hung up his phone. It was 6pm in California and he felt like celebrating.

Shanghai

Li Ming's aunt was pleased with her room. The agents were very kind and treated her like family. They ate with her and enjoyed some of her home cooking. They had been more than willing to shop for the groceries needed to make the dishes.

She had worried about Li Ming. Was she safe? Were they treating her badly? She had no way of knowing. The call was short, but it helped her anxiety. She was hopping Li Ming would call again soon.

The main agent was a man of about fifty years of age. He had lived all of his life in Shanghai. He had two children, both grown and with their own families. He understood the worry she felt.

A lab in North Korea

Li Ming walked back into the lab. She saw Dauen was working on a box of parts that had just arrived.

While she took her time walking back to her work bench, she thought about the conversation with her aunt. *What was my aunt trying to tell me?* She went back over the conversation. Her favorite book was missing. The one she read daily. She really did not have a favorite book and she certainly couldn't remember reading daily. Daily or Daley. *Was she trying to tell me that she was with Susan Daley.* The only book I can remember being my favorite was *The four horsemen of the Apocalypse* She stopped mid step. The men holding her aunt were gone. She was safe with Susan Daley. *Wow, this changes things. Kwang and his partner would not be able to threaten me with harm to my aunt.*

Li Ming looked around to see if anyone was watching her. Of course they were, she was on the surveillance system. She walked up to her bench and smiled at Dauen. "Are all the parts we ordered here?"

"Yes, they are all here" said Dauen. She looked down and did not smile.

"Thank you Dauen. Place each of the parts with the sub-assemblies. We can then start installing them. Have you checked with the machine shop to when the focus coil would be ready?"

"Yes, they said it would be ready next Wednesday." Li Ming smiled at Dauen. There was no response. She continued her task of sorting out the parts.

Li Ming entered a few equations into her computer terminal. She was sure it was being monitored. She went through the calculations and found one flaw in a voltage reading. She worked for over two hours adjusting the components that were controlling the voltage. It finally stabilized.

A man came up with a large package. He placed it on the bench and left. Li Ming looked at Dauen. "I didn't order anything else. I don't know what this is" said Dauen.

Li Ming used a screw driver to slice the tape and open the package. To her surprise it was a new oscilloscope, a Hewlett Packard. That was really great. Someone knew the old equipment on the shelf did not have the fine tuning needed to calibrate the ion flow precisely. She looked around the lab. No one seemed a bit interested. She shrugged and placed the new device on her bench.

The bell rang for lunch. She and Dauen had packed their own lunches and went to the small break room to eat. They sat in silence for a while.

"Dauen, if you can give me the phone number for your sister, I'll ask Kwang if you can check on your family."

Dauen looked in horror at Li Ming. "No, they will get mad and might hurt my husband. Thank you but I don't want them to think I am not loyal."

Li Ming nodded she understood. There had to be a way to get information about her family. *Maybe I'll do a little threatening of my own.*

Chapter 18

Pasadena FBI Office

William had all of his agents in the small conference room. Some had to stand. "People, we have been given a directive to continue with the Cal Tech case. I do not have our assignment yet, but the Deputy Director will be addressing us shortly. I will hazard a guess this has something to do with national security. I want all of us to give the director our full attention."

As if on cue, the conference phone rang. William pressed the answer button. "Director you are on the speaker phone. All of the agents are here."

"Thank you William. Ladies and gentlemen, we have been asked by the intelligence community to assist in a case of national security. You all know that a top secret device was stolen from Cal Tech. You know the mole was totally unaware of what she was doing. Because it is a national security item, I can not reveal the device's function at this time. I can say to you that the entire world is at risk. We know the North Koreans have the device and we know they have kidnapped one of the Cal Tech scientists in an attempt to make the device work. Because of the importance of this case, all of you will be signing a document that binds you to the national security acts and rules. Are there any questions?"

William looked around the room. They all sat in silence. "Sir there are no questions", said William.

"Good. Agent Braun will be briefed on the assignments and will be speaking to each of you on your role. People this is as important as it gets. Thanks and good luck." The phone went silent.

William stood and looked at his team. "Please take one of the documents on the table and sign it. I will have all the teams planned and names assigned with the specific details of each team's objectives by 0700. Any questions?" There were none. "Okay, dismissed."

William returned to his office. It was late. He phoned his wife and told her he was going to be late and not to wait up for him. He checked his secure email account. The Deputy Director had sent the full briefing. Each team was assigned a specific target. The fake organization was to be completely investigated and diagrammed; the man apprehended at the dead drop is to be interrogated thoroughly to find his contacts. One team will do a complete background check on the secretary and her lab employer. The last team is to determine how the North Koreans obtained a key to the equipment room and trace the manufacturer of the video device left behind that was used to fool the security people monitoring the lab building. There was a private message to William directing him to make every effort possible to get hard evidence that North Korea was in fact responsible for the theft. William completed his list of personnel and assignments. He left the office at 11:38.

The lab, North Korea

A uniformed guard approached Li Ming and Dauen. He told them it was time to go home. The day was over. They had been at the lab bench working for over 10 hours. Dauen told the guard they would have to shut down all of their equipment before they could leave. He stood and waited. It took about ten minutes to shut down all the devices.

They followed the guard to the same car that had brought them earlier in the day. It seemed like a week to Li Ming. She had been thinking of how to get a message to Dauen's family. Nothing yet was workable. The ride to their apartment building was short. She carefully observed the streets and landmarks.

A man in a suit met them in the lobby and accompanied them to their door. Dauen opened the door to their unit. He remained in the hall. They entered and went to their respective rooms. Each changed into lounging wear, which Li Ming thought was not too unlike the day time wear.

"What would you like to have for dinner", said Dauen. It was the first time all day she had initiated a conversation.

Li Ming smiled and hugged Dauen. The simple act of a hug perked Dauen up. "Let's have chicken and rice with spice cakes for desert", said Li Ming.

Dauen clapped her hands. "Just what I was wanting." She went to the cupboard and took out a bag of rice and began to prepare the pot of water to cook the rice.

Li Ming went to the small refrigerator and took out a package of cut up chicken. It was the only meat they had purchased the day before. "We will have to purchase more supplies. I don't have any money. How are we to do the shopping?"

"They gave me some money when I arrived. I will ask Kwang tomorrow", said Dauen.

"Do you know if we have any days off work", asked Li Ming.

"Kwang told me we work ten days and have one day off."

Li Ming looked at Dauen and smiled. "Then we have to ask someone to purchase some items for us until we have our day off."

They cooked dinner together and ate with gusto. They had worked hard all day and lunch was not filling. They did not talk much. Mostly about some of the tests that they were conducting on the power supply. They knew every word was being recorded.

Dauen turned on the TV. There were only three channels. Two were party channels with propaganda messages. The other channel had a news program followed with a classical music program. She left it on that channel. The music filled the apartment and gave a festive atmosphere to an otherwise dull evening. They read for a while and both turned in at 2200.

Shanghai MSS Office

Jai Chun returned from the abandoned air field and had his top agents come to his office. The entire situation was a disaster. There were foreign agents running all over the place, shooting people and none of his agents had a clue as to what was happening.

"I want all of you to listen carefully. There will be no repeat of this situation. You are to know everything going on in our country. Every foreign agent is to be watched. Every person entering or leaving China is to be checked. Every incident of the police is to be cross checked with other incidents for a possible pattern. I will not have anyone on my staff that cannot adhere to this policy. Is that clear?" No one spoke.

"I am meeting with the Americans again this afternoon. We will decide what we will be doing with regards to the North Koreans. We now have a reasonably good report that the North Koreans are in fact behind the bazaar events that have taken place on our soil. The Americans have been forth coming and honest in their reports. We will give them every opportunity to assist us in the case. They lost four of their agents. That is unacceptable. I want your teams on the case immediately. You are to give me a written report every morning before 0800. You are dismissed." No one spoke. They each left the office and went to their respective areas. They knew Jai was not making idle threats; their jobs were on the line.

Shanghai US Consulate, CIA office

Susan Daley began the day with a phone call to her boss in Langley, Virginia. It was not a pleasant conversation. She was told that the FBI was included in the case along with the NSA and the Department of Defense. She was to make every effort to penetrate the North Korean spy organization in China. Nothing was said about including the Chinese in these pursuits. She hung up the secure satellite phone and stared at her desk top for several minutes.

"Excuse me madam", said Nu. Susan looked up and waved him into her office.

"Good morning Nu, any good news?" She looked with anticipation at Nu.

"I have heard back from my contact in North Korea. Dr. Wu is living in a state apartment building with a young woman. The building is well guarded but not like the lab. My contact has access to the area and will be bursting a file with pictures this afternoon. We will also get a background check on the young woman with Dr. Wu."

"That is good news Nu. I will be in a conference with Jai Chun later today. You are to come to my office at 1730 hours."

"I will be here", said Nu. He left her office for his cubical at the other side of the large open room. He knew that having Jai Chun here exposed himself to being recognized in the future. He had actually met Chun several times in Beijing. He doubted if Jai Chun would remember him. This was a strange case and he was sure it would get stranger yet.

The day went by without any unusual events. Susan was in her office most of the day with team captains popping in and out. At 1700 she closed all the documents that were open on her desktop. She shut down her computer and switched off her cell phone. She did not want to be disturbed during this conference with Jai Chun.

Nu Lee went to Susan's office promptly at 1730 hours. In less than a minute a man was being led to Susan's office. Jai Chun came into Susan's office did a shallow bow to both Susan and Nu. He sat down and made himself comfortable. He waited until Susan spoke first.

"Jai, I would like for you to meet my agent in charge of our Shanghai group, Nu Lee."

"Susan, Nu, thank you for inviting me here to discuss the situation. Again I wish to express how sorry I am on your loss. He waited a few seconds to continue. Nu and I have met on several occasions in Beijing." Susan's eyebrows went up. Nu smiled and nodded.

"Well let's get down to business", said Susan. "Have your people confirmed all that we spoke about in your office?" Susan watched his face very carefully.

"Yes, you were correct in your report. Every detail is being examined as we speak. I have teams following up on each incident. We think we know where Dr. Wu was taken before her transfer to the airplane. It is an old abandoned railway repair depot near your safe house. There was no evidence they had been using the place for very long. We have not been able to tie any of those arrested to the North Koreans. It appears they used hired operatives from local crime families. We are checking to see if the heads of these families have any ties to North Korea. My agent that is with your men who are guarding Dr. Wu's aunt reported that a phone call came in and Dr. Wu spoke to her aunt. Was any progress made to locate the source of the call?"

"Thank you for that report Jai. We have made some progress. We are ninety percent sure that we know exactly where Dr. Wu is being forced to work on the stolen device. We will have more information by morning. We also had her aunt read a short script that contained vague mentions of the fact the aunt is not under the control of the North Koreans We were unable to confirm if Dr. Wu understood the coded message. It seems the device was stolen without its power supply. So it's like stealing a car with no engine." They all laughed at this analogy. Nu sat without speaking. He was very interested in what might be going through Jai Chun's mind. He was certain that the politicos would not be happy. Chun was high up but expendable.

"Susan, we would like to propose that each of your teams be paired with one of our teams to facilitate the use of all our resources."

"I think that is a great idea. If we cooperate then it would make the job go faster and we won't have to keep meeting like this." They laughed. Nu raised his hand."Nu please speak", said Susan.

"I would like to work with Minister Chun's team looking into the North Korean's network in China. It would give us a good idea of what targets may be selected if they got the device working." Susan smiled and nodded. Chun sat without any facial expression.

"Jai, what do you say to that proposal. With us pooling our information on the North Koreans, it should shorten the time it will take to map their organization."

"Susan, Nu, I will take the proposal under advisement. I must give my people a chance to raise any questions about our joint effort. I will be back to you before noon tomorrow."

"That's fair enough", said Susan. "Thank you for your time coming here and may we work together with good intentions." Jai Chun stood and shook hands with Nu and Susan. One of Nu's staff led Minister Chun out of the building.

Susan turned and pointed at Nu. "Why didn't you tell me you had met Jai Chun?"

"I was working under-cover as an embassy staff member. On several occasions Chun attended affairs and functions that I was assigned. I would not have thought he would remember. I have to give him credit, he doesn't miss much."

"Yes, we have just learned a lesson. Never take for granted anything in this business."

Chapter 19

North Korea Lab

Li Ming and Dauen worked all morning on the power supply. It was not going well. It was obvious that the input voltage was not steady and was not within the limits of the filters. "Dauen, check with someone and get us two new filters 300 farads and a 40 henry choke coil."

Dauen nodded and went to the lab office with the request. The man in charge of the lab phoned someone and told Dauen the parts would be delivered early in the afternoon. Dauen returned to the work bench. "He says this afternoon."

Li Ming knew that getting the input voltage smoothed out would make the power supply partially functional. She saw Kwang walking towards her. He had a determined look on his face.

"Dr. Wu, you are not meeting the time schedule. What is the reason?"

Li Ming turned and stared. "We have built the power supply. Unfortunately the parts are not of the quality to stabilize the input. We have ordered new parts to hopefully correct the unstable input voltage. The parts are due this afternoon. There is nothing I can do about the input voltage being so unstable."

Kwang nodded and returned to his temporary office. He was not a happy camper. Kwang knew that his boss did not want to hear excuses, especially any that highlighted the inferior quality of North Korean products. He would have to be very careful in how he explained the delay. He opened a drawer and took out the satellite phone. He pressed the call button. A man answered.

"Is the woman able to speak?" He listened for a few seconds. "I will be calling you later this afternoon. Have her ready to speak on the phone." He abruptly hung up. He had to put more pressure on Dr. Wu.

He was determined to force Li Ming to work faster and complete the power supply. Seok Dong-Suk was not a patient man.

Shanghai US Consulate, CIA office

The satellite phone rang. An agent typed several key strokes on a laptop computer connected to the phone and answered.

"Have the woman available to speak on the phone later this afternoon. Is she unharmed?" The man assured the caller she was fine and would be available late in the afternoon. The call was terminated.

The agent picked up a phone and called Susan Daley's office.

"This is Susan." She listened carefully to the report and a playback of the conversation. "Well it seems they still believe they have Mrs. Wang under their control." Susan smiled and felt the day had started as good as it could get.

North Korea lab

The parts arrived at 1400 hours. Dauen opened the box and removed the parts. Li Ming examined them carefully. "Test this capacitor and determine if it is a full 300 Farads. I will test the coil. If they are within ninety-five percent then we can make the input voltage stable enough to activate the power supply.

They worked for over two hours testing the parts. They appeared to be within the tolerances required by Li Ming. She was in the process of installing a choke coil when Kwang came up and asked her to follow him to the office.

Kwang and Li Ming were the only two in the room. Kwang opened the drawer and removed the sat phone. He pressed the call button. After three rings the phone was answered. "Put the woman on the phone." He waited several seconds before he heard the woman's voice. "Your niece is not cooperating. She is far behind our schedule. You will tell her to get on schedule." He listened for a few seconds and handed the phone to Li Ming.

"Hello aunt. Are you unharmed?" She listened to her aunt carefully. "Yes I do miss you", said Li Ming. "I also miss my daily reading. I will try to catch up the work here to meet their schedule. Maybe in a week I will be caught up." She hoped they understood that in a week the device would be operational for testing.

Kwang reached and took the phone. Put my man on the phone. The aunt handed the phone to the agent. Kwang heard the agent's hello. "You are to tie up the woman and no food or water until I call back." He terminated the call and stared at Li Ming.

"I am doing the best I can. I want to speak to my aunt first thing tomorrow morning. If she has been harmed, not fed or is tied up, I will stop work. Do you understand? You can do anything to me, but if she is harmed in anyway, you will get no work from me." She looked Kwang in the eye. She got up and left Kwang seated at the table with a shocked look on his face.

Li Ming wanted to skip across the room, but knew she had to keep the fact that her aunt was safe a secret for now. She now had leverage over Kwang.

Kwang sat for some time thinking. *Maybe the leverage over her aunt is not working. This young lady has guts. She could cause all sorts of problems for me if the aunt is harmed. I can't put physical persuasion on Li Ming; we have to have the device up and running very soon.*

Kwang took out the phone and punched in the number for Shanghai. The phone was answered on the second ring. "Untie the woman and make sure she is treated well. Feed her and make sure she gets rest." He listened for a response. "Yes, those are your orders. I will be calling tomorrow morning checking on her." He pressed the end key.

Shanghai US Consulate, CIA office

Susan had been in the room monitoring the conversation. She heard Li Ming confirm the message. She knew that daily was Daley. She had told them that in one week they would try to energize the device. They now had some leverage.

Li Ming's aunt turned to Susan. "What are we to do next?" asked Mrs. Wang.

"At the moment, we do nothing. We will have more information tomorrow morning", said Susan.

The sat phone rang again. The agent answered on the second ring. He listened for several seconds. "Yes sir. I will do as you instruct." The call was terminated and he put the phone down.

Susan smiled at what she had just heard."Well it appears that he has had a change of heart for Mrs. Wang. I speculate that Li Ming has dug her heels in and will refuse to work if you are harmed, not fed or in stress."

Washington, D.C.

The director of the NSA sat and listened to the Secretary of Defense and the CIA director argue the strategy for extracting Dr. Wu. The Defense Department wanted to control the extraction using a Seal Team. The CIA wanted to use their covert operatives. The argument continued for several minutes. No one budged.

"Gentlemen, it may help if we can coordinate a joint effort", said the NSA director. "It appears you both have teams capable of the extraction. I suggest you two combine your teams into specialties needed to make the extraction.

The CIA director sat back and stared at the NSA director. The Secretary of Defense looked over at the CIA director.

"I will agree to that. The two teams must have a joint strategy that assures us that the extraction can take place with minimum exposure and damage", said the Secretary of Defense. The CIA director nodded agreement

The NSA director leaned forward, "I will offer our two satellites. We can link up with the Defense Department systems in a matter of hours to provide real-time communications. Let's meet back here tomorrow and go over the strategy."

The three men nodded agreements. They stood and shook hands and each left the meeting to make it happen.

Norfolk, Virginia

Admiral Johnson sat with his SEAL team commanders. He had arrived back in Norfolk only an hour ago from a top secret meeting with the Secretary of Defense.

"Men, this meeting is top secret and a matter of national security. It doesn't get any higher than this. We are going to work with the CIA team Blue Belt to do an extraction from North Korea." He waited for the disclosure to sink-in. "The leader of the CIA team is here and I will introduce you in a moment. I want you to come up with a joint strategy to extract a woman scientist that the North Koreans kidnapped from Shanghai a few days ago. Each of your teams have specialized skills. You are to build a special team with the CIA people that can do the job." The admiral looked around the table. He was very proud of his SEAL commanders. He got up and went to the door and motioned for someone to come in.

Shree Webster, a woman with beauty queen features, 44 years old with short dark hair in a pixie cut and dressed in a smart business suit came through the door. For over ten years she commanded the elite covert CIA team Blue Belt. The admiral looked at the faces of his team commanders and smiled.

"Gentlemen I'd like to introduce you to Commander Webster. She commands the CIA team. Commander please have a seat." She sat in a space between two of the SEAL commanders. Commander Webster looked around the table and nodded at each of the five commanders.

Admiral Johnson cleared his throat, "Teams, we have one of the hardest jobs I've ever been associated with. This extraction will be one of extreme difficulty. We know where the subject is, we know the security surrounding her and we also know the importance of time. The clock is ticking on a matter that could throw us into a world-wide situation like none you ever dreamed of. So, I will leave you to come up with a plan. The details of the case are in this folder." He placed the folder on the table and left the room.

One of the senior commanders of the SEAL teams stood. Gentlemen and lady, I suggest we elect a lead commander to this group. "I nominate Jon Ferguson." He sat down. No one spoke.

Shree looked around the table. "Gentlemen, I don't know anything about you and would like for each of you to tell me about your teams and what you consider is your team's specialty."

Jon Ferguson stood. "I'm Jon Ferguson. My team is trained on stealth insertion. That's when a team is inserted without any evidence of ever being present. It sounds easy but is one of the most difficult actions to be carried out successfully." He sat down.

The man next to him stood. He had bright red hair that was cropped very short, giving him sort of halo effect. My name is Harold Stoner and my team is trained in compact explosives., which means to blow something up with the least amount of material. We use shaped charges to accomplish most of our missions."

The next man stood. "I'm Tony Masters. My team is trained in communications. We capture all missions in real-time. We were the team on the ground during the capture of several high value targets in Pakistan. I'm not at liberty to say who, but some of you know."

The next man stood. "I'm Henry Bryant. My team is trained in escape techniques. This involves providing a safe path to pull teams out of enemy stronghold positions. We use high tech means to plot a safe passage and provide remote cover fire if necessary." He nodded and sat down.

The last of the group stood."I'm Al Hughes. My team has been trained for close urban assault. This involves using the urban structure to our advantage. We specialize in stealth and speed. We usually are involved in capture or termination of high value targets.

Shree stood. "I'm Shree Webster. "The Blue Belt team is trained in extraction techniques. These include modes of transportation, communications and decommissioning of high explosives. Our team has been deployed mostly in the Middle East. We have several members who were born in South Korea and speak fluent Korean. That is one of the reasons why my team was selected to join your group. We are currently in training at Camp Pendleton.

Harold Stoner stood. "Commanders, I would like to call for an end of nominations and call for the election of Jon Ferguson as our leader.

Everyone nodded agreement. "Then let's see the hands of all in favor of electing Jon to be our leader", said Harold. There was a unanimous vote.

Commander Ferguson stood. "Commanders, we are ordered to come up with a strategy and detail plan for extracting someone from a city in North Korea. We must put away territorial differences and egos to accomplish this. Let's get started." He opened the folder on the table.

Chapter 20

Norfolk, Virginia

Jon Ferguson opened the folder the Admiral had placed on the table. Inside was a USB drive, a folded map, several pictures and narratives. "People, we have a location. It is named Sungmim. According to the NSA, this is a special zone established for high tech labs and factories. It is where North Korea's nuclear laboratories are located" He shuffled through the documents "Harold, grab one of those laptops and plug in this USB drive"

As soon as the laptop was activated, a large flat screen TV displayed the desktop. The USB drive displayed a list of contents. Jon read one of the documents. "This says to open a folder labeled NK23."

Harold double clicked on the folder NK23. The screen immediately displayed a detailed map of North Korea.

"Harold, zoom in on the city Sungmim." The image was not unlike a Google Earth display. The city was laid out in perfect square blocks. There was a river on the East side and low mountains on the North side.

The group studied the city layout carefully. A small red x appeared near the East side. There were six low rise buildings near the x. The buildings were in a campus like area. There appeared to be a high wall surrounding the six buildings. Guard stations could be made out along the wall. "You have to admit the NSA have some amazing technology", said Jon. Commander Webster raised her hand. "Yes, Commander."

"Sir, how old is this data?"

"Commander, according to the fine print on the bottom of the screen, it has yesterday's date and time", said Harold.

"Sorry, I can't see the fine print. Too old I guess." The group laughed.

Jon moved to the wall with the screen. "Group, let's break down our project into the overall picture, and go down to details from there.

First, can we safely get a team into North Korea without causing World War Three? Let's hear some ideas."

Commander Webster raised her hand. She got the nod to continue from Jon. "From what I see, we have three choices, Land, Sea or Air. Air would be almost impossible to get in without detection. Land would require hundreds of miles to get a team in safely undetected from all the check points. The sea offers the best route from a China launch point. The river Taedong may be a way to get in with minimum over land travel. We will need detail info on the river, depth, width, patrols and detection devices. I see there is a bridge across the entrance. This may pose a problem."

Jon paced back and forth in front of the giant TV screen. "People, it appears the approach from the sea is the only viable choice. If we can get the Chinese to agree to allow us to launch from one of their seaports, then we must concentrate on how to get across a very large area undetected." Jon saw Tony raise his hand.

"I think if we can get some help from any operatives' already in North Korea then we could plan how to use them to achieve our goal," said Tony.

They bounced several ideas on the sea transport from rubber rafts to fishing boats. The discussion lasted well into the late afternoon. "Folks, we are beating a dead horse. Let's take a dinner break and meet back here at 1900 hours", said Jon. They all agreed and filed out to the cafeteria. Three Marine guards were posted at the door to the conference room and hallway.

Jon made his way to the admiral's office. The admiral was busy with someone. His aid said that it would be only a few more minutes. Jon decided to wait.

The door to the admiral's office opened and the admiral was escorting a tall civilian. The man made no eye contact with Jon and left through the outer door. The admiral waved Jon into this office.

"Sir, the group have asked me to be the lead on our venture. We need some assistance from the CIA or the NSA on assets available on the ground in North Korea. The group consensus is that we will need considerable help in getting from the coast to the extraction zone. We also will need help with getting the Chinese to allow our team to launch from their shores." The admiral listened very carefully. He opened a drawer in his desk and took out a top secret secure phone. He pressed a button.

"Sir, we need assistance in our strategy. Several questions have emerged regarding cooperation with the Chinese and assets that may be available in North Korea. Do you have anyone that help?" The admiral listened for over a minute. "Yes sir. I will make the arrangements. Good bye." He put the phone back into his desk.

"Jon, we will have someone that can answer most of those question here tomorrow. I suggest that your group assume all the questions to be positive until that person shows up." Jon got up and saluted the admiral and left for dinner in the cafeteria.

The cafeteria was on the second floor. He walked up the two flights of stairs. A Marine guard stood at the door to the cafeteria. "Sir, may I see your ID?" Jon took his ID from his pocket and handed it to the guard. The guard compared the ID picture and checked his name on a clipboard. He handed the ID back and saluted.

Jon. was impressed with the security that was put in place within the last few hours. The admiral was not taking any chances.

He saw his group sitting together on the far side of the cafeteria and the civilian that had left the admiral's office a short time ago sitting a few tables away. He waved at the group as he made his way to the serving line. He went through the line and picked up his tray at the cashier. The cashier said the admiral said the meal was on the house. He made his way to his group. He noticed the civilian sitting a few tables away but he did not look up as Jon went by.

Pasadena

William's phone rang. He recognized the caller ID. "This is William." He looked at the time in Washington and was surprised the deputy director was working this late. The conversation was short. He was told to get to the airport immediately. A private FBI jet was waiting for him. He would be gone for twenty-four hours. No need to pack anything. The deputy director informed William that further information would be given to him on the plane.

William put the phone down. He called his wife. After twenty years, she was accustomed to his sudden change of plans.

He drove to the Pasadena airport. His instructions were to drive to the air freight terminal. The plane would be there. He parked his car in a small parking area at the side of the air freight hanger. When he arrived and parked, he saw a sleek G4 jet with the door open and two people waiting at the bottom of the stairs.

William walked swiftly to the waiting plane. The pilot introduced himself. He shook hands with William. He introduced the other man as an agent from the Denver office, Dan Patterson. They went up the stairs. There was no one else in the passenger compartment.

William could see into the cockpit. The copilot was going through the check list for takeoff. The pilot went into the cockpit and closed the door. The engines wined as they spun up. The plane was air-born within a minute.

"William, the deputy director has authorized me and you to disclose all we know about the North Korean case to the team assembled to extract Dr. Wu." Dan Patterson waited for William to ask a question.

"Where are we going", asked William.

"We are headed to Norfolk to assist in a plan to extract Dr. Wu. Your contact with the CIA office in Shanghai is essential to the planning. I was informed about your team's work on the North Korean theft of some device from Cal Tech. It is very important that we try to directly tie the North Koreans to the theft."

William knew all of this from his phone call with the deputy director. "Yes, I am fully briefed on the directive from the deputy director. What is your role?" William was not sure why this agent was involved.

"I am charged with coordination between the FBI, the CIA, The Department of Defense and the NSA. They met in Washington and agreed to make this a joint effort of the entire intelligence community."

William sat back in his seat. He was not happy with being jerked around the world, First China, then Pasadena and now Norfolk. He had not informed his team he would be away. "I need to inform my team that I will be away tomorrow. Is there a phone available?"

"Yes, there is one in your arm rest."

William opened the arm rest and removed the phone. He tapped in the number to his office. "Hi April, I will be away tomorrow. Let the team captains know if they need me for anything to call my cell phone." He waited for a response. "Thank you." He pressed the end button and replaced the phone into the arm rest. It was going to be a busy day tomorrow.

Chapter 21

Virginia Beach, Virginia

The FBI plane landed at Oceania Naval Air Station at 0730 local time. A car was waiting and whisked the two agents to a building on the far side of the base.

The car door and was opened by a Marine captain. "Sirs if you will come with me." the captain opened the door to the lobby. Several armed Marines were stationed at each door.

The Marine captain stopped and entered a code and stared into a device on the wall. The door clicked open. They entered a large office with a Major sitting at a desk with a computer screen. He motioned for the two agents to enter. He opened a door that led to the admiral's office. .The admiral got up and met the men as they walked into his office. The major closed the door.

"Gentlemen, thanks' for coming. We have six team commanders brainstorming strategy at the moment. They have many questions that I think the two of you can supply answers. Please follow the captain to the conference room." The two agents said nothing as the captain motioned for them to follow him to a door behind the admiral's desk. The door opened to a short hallway. Two armed marines stood guard outside the door. One opened the door for the two agents.

The captain introduced the agents to the group and left the room.

Jon was standing near the large TV and introduced himself as the elected chairman of the group. "Dan and William please find a seat. I am sure you have been briefed on what we're planning. We have a few questions. Let's get the major questions answered first. Commander Hughes has a list of questions from the group."

Al Hughes stood and read from a document. "We have determined that the insert must be by sea. That means we have to launch from China. Can we get approval from China to launch our extract team from one of their seaports?"

Dan turned to William. "William is familiar with the current relationship with China."

William stood. "Gentlemen and lady, when I left China a meeting had taken place between our CIA station chief and the head of the MSS. They are cooperating fully. The last conversation I had with the station chief indicated they were pooling their teams in an effort to be more efficient and improve communications. I believe China will welcome our extraction team, but be prepared to have one or more of their personnel join your team."

"Does that mean we have to accept their personnel or it's a no deal?" asked Henry Bryant.

"I will have to speak to the station chief to be sure, but I would think they would want to be part of the extraction. It is their country and we are their guest. Will this put the project at risk? I don't know, but I would wager they have some highly trained people. They may even have assets within North Korea. He sat down.

Jon looked at his team members. "Look guys let's take this one step at a time. First we need a plan, next we need to evaluate team requirements and lastly we need to assemble the team. You will be leaving here at noon tomorrow for the West Coast. We will assemble the teams there. We will leave the next day for Shanghai. So time is of the essence. Are there more questions for William and Dan?"

Al nodded yes. "William, can you give us any information on Dr. Wu. Age, physical condition and anything else you think should be considered in our plans?"

Dan stood. He handed Jon a USB drive. A picture of Li Ming appeared on the TV. "As you see, Dr. Wu is in her late twenties and is very fit. She is extremely intelligent as you might surmise. She is approximately five feet eight inches in height. She is tall for an Asian and weighs about 120 pounds with short black hair."

"Thank you," said Jon. "What do we know about her accommodations?"

"We know the building and some of the security deployed. We are expecting more information sometime today. The asset in North Korea is not physically able to get many of the details. It is my understanding the asset is in advanced age. The NSA is attempting to get us as much Intel via satellite as possible. This information should be available later today", said Dan. "As soon as we get the Intel, we'll share it."

Jon walked to the head of the table. "Here are some things we need to know. (1) The best location to launch the teams. (2) Security Intel on the approach to the Taedong River basin. (3) The best place to disembark the teams. (4) Detail map of the streets and building approaching the target building. (5) Any assistance from within North Korea. William if you can work on items one through 4, and Dan if you can find out the answer to item five."

"I will have you answers by 1700." Dan and William left the room and were escorted by one of the armed Marines to a small office down the hall.

"You may use this office. It has an encrypted phone and computer. Let me know if you need anything else." The Marine closed the door and returned to his station.

"I will send a message to Susan Daley now with the first four questions. I will also enquire if the Chinese will insist on placing men within our teams", said William. He opened Microsoft Word and typed the message. He then ran the file through the encryption program on an FBI server in Washington. He attached the encrypted file to an email addressed to Susan Daley. The email was routed through Langley's server farm. Susan would receive the message within three minutes.

Dan picked up the receiver of the encrypted phone and entered a ten digit number. He listened as the phone buzzed. "Sir, we are in Virginia Beach with the teams. They want to know if there can be any reliable assistance on the ground at the target area." Dan pulled a yellow pad over and wrote some information. "Yes sir. I will ask him to contact them now." He pressed the end key.

William was completing his email when Dan hung up the phone. "Who am I to contact?"

"Here is the number for the encrypted phone. It is our contact at the CIA. They are expecting your call."

William pulled the phone over and put the number in for the contact. The phone was answered on the first ring. "This is William Braun; I understand you are expecting my call." He listened. "Yes, we are with the extraction teams now. They would like as much assistance from any assets on the ground as possible." William looked over at Dan and frowned. "I see. Okay I understand." He hung up. "Well according to that guy, they have no one available to assist."

Dan made another call. "This is Dan. Has any new Intel come in on the target area?" Dan made a note and passed it to William. It read, NSA is sending an encrypted report as we speak. Dan listened for another minute and hung up the phone. "Check your bureau email for a report document. It seems they hit the jackpot on the river information and the street maps of Sungmim.

William brought up the bureau web site and typed in his password for email. A document was attached to a short memo. He download-ed the document and ran it through the encryption program. A four page document appeared in the output file. He opened the document. "Wow, I don't think the group is going to be thrilled with this."

Shanghai

Susan's computer beeped indicating an email had arrived. She opened the email and noted it was from William Braun. She read the questions. She reread the questions especially the one about the pos-sibility that the Chinese may insist on placing their men within the extraction team. She made a call to Jai Chun.

"Jai, this is Susan. I have heard from our extraction team. They have several questions and I think we need to have a meeting with your team." She listened for a moment. "Yes, I can come to your office. I will be there in an hour." She hung up the phone. She went to Nu's cubical in the back of the room.

"Hi boss. What can I do for you?"

"Nu, we have to go meet with Jai Chun's team. Bring anything you feel will help. A picture of Li Ming and the NSA observations." He nodded yes and began to collect a few folders. He downloaded a pic-ture of Li Ming to a USB thumb drive along with the NSA file.

Susan and Nu were driven to the MSS office in the insurance build-ing. Nu was not surprised at the destination. "Madam, I have not met my team looking into the North Korean spy network. Maybe this will be an opportunity." Susan didn't respond but was observing several people who appeared to be loitering in front of the building.

"It appears Jai has beefed up his security." She motioned at the rather obvious gathering of agents in front of the building. She opened the door and stepped out. One of the men immediately stepped forward and motioned for Nu and her to follow him. They went directly to the elevator and up to Jai's office. The MSS agent did not stay with them.

"Susan and Nu, welcome. Please follow me to the conference room." They walked across the room to a door with a guard. The guard bowed to them and opened the door. Susan counted nine people seated at the table. They all rose and bowed as they came into the room. "Please be seated" said Jai. There were three empty chairs. Nu and Susan sat down.

Jai remained standing. He moved to a flat screen TV. "Ms. Daley and Nu Lee are here to share information on this case. I will ask Ms Daley to inform us."

Susan remained seated. "I have received information that an extraction team is being prepared as we speak. They have requested some information." Susan opened a folder. "They need as much info as possible on the best place to launch the team from your shores. They also need as much info on the Taedong River basin as possible. Patrols, detection devices and types of traffic such as container ships, fishing boats and military craft coming and going will aid them. " She looked along the table, each person was taking notes."They have requested any Intel on the best place to land and approach the target. And lastly, do you have any assets on the ground to assist in making this successful?"

Susan turned to Nu. "Mr. Lee has some Intel we would like to share.

"I will need a laptop computer connected to the TV." A young woman immediately went to a cabinet and removed a Dell laptop and connected it to the TV with a HDMI cable. "Thank you." He handed the USB thumb drive to her. She inserted the drive and sat down.

"The photo's you are looking at were taken by satellite yesterday. As you can see there was a bit of overcast and the picture quality is not good, but you can make out the building we have designated as the main target." The picture changed to one of a compound of buildings with a large wall surrounding it. "Here is the lab where Dr. Wu is forced to work on the device the North Koreans stole from Cal Tech. You can see the guard stations along the wall. We do not think we can breach these fortifications. The extraction team would like to get in and out without firing a shot and if possible undetected. They will have a long way back to the Chinese mainland after the extraction. If they are detected before reaching the open sea, then it reduces the possibility of a successful extraction." The next slide was a picture of Li Ming. "This is Dr. Wu. You may copy this picture to your machine and print copies for all to memorize."

Jai was standing to the side. His face did not show any signs. "People, this is the type of Intel we need. Each of you have your own assignments. I would like you to prepare a report that best answers all of the questions Ms Daley and Mr. Lee have asked, especially the Intel on the landing point and the river security systems. You should have this information readily at hand. You are dismissed for one hour to prepare your reports."

Susan watched as the group got up to leave. "Jai, may I ask the team investigating the North Korean spy network to remain."

"Yes. Kow please remain." A middle aged man nodded and sat back down. The door closed and the four were the only remaining occupants.

Jai Chun introduced Kow to Susan and Nu. "Nu I remember your request to work with our counter Intel group. Kow is the team leader. Please ask any questions."

"Mr. Kow, I may have some Intel your group may not be up-to-date on." Jai's face showed surprise.

"Nu please share that information." Jai watched as Nu opened a folder on the USB drive. He started a slide show of six pictures. Each was of an agent that the CIA had identified as North Korean RBG agents. The last picture was of a woman. "This is their station chief. She is responsible for the design of the kidnapping of Dr. Wu. She actually was with the team that invaded our safe house. She is ruthless in her execution of orders. She did not go with Dr. Wu to North Korea." Our informant has been one hundred percent correct in the past. We have no reason not to accept this at face value."

Jai was stunned. His people did not have any information on the woman. She looked familiar but he couldn't place her face. Kow was staring at the woman's picture. He had a shocked look.

"Kow, do you know who this?" Jai leaned over the table into Kow's face.

Kow swallowed. "I think this is Madam Wo. She is the director of the Beijing opera company. She is well known in political circles."

Jai's face was screwed up as if he had bitten a lemon. "I want every scrap of information you can gather on Madam Wo. Go get it now!" Kow quickly got up and bowed to Jai and left the room. "Nu, there is no doubt you will be welcomed to our counter intelligence team." He pulled a chair out and sat down with an exhausted look on his face.

Jai was thinking. *I don't know how to report this to the President. His wife is one of the patrons of the opera. She will know Madam Wo personally. This is going to be disastrous.*

Chapter 22

Virginia Beach, Virginia

The teams took their seats around the table after lunch. Most had discussed various scenarios during lunch. All had extensive experience in the field.

Jon called the group to order. All chatter ceased. "People we are up against the clock. As you know, we normally have several weeks to prepare and practice an extraction. This time, we will not have the luxury of practice. The latest Intel from our station chief arrived during lunch. William will bring us up-to-date."

William stood and handed a USB drive to Jon. "We have received answers to all but one of the questions. The document you see before you is the email we received from Shanghai during lunch. The question relative to the Taedong River and basin is here.

As you can see there are many patrol boats, aircraft and underwater detection devices. All of the ships entering into the basin are stopped by patrol boats and boarded for inspection. There are no exceptions. The aircraft fly over the basin in a varying pattern. So there is no way to plot any path. The river itself is lined with sonar detection devices. The river is quite deep at the entrance into the basin with an average depth of seventy feet." William looked around the table. The commanders all took notes.

"The best spot to launch from China is from the port of Dalian. It is 166 nautical miles from the mouth of the basin. There is a military airport at Dalian. The distance from Shanghai to Dalian is 539 air miles." William opened another folder. "This information is from the MSS. Their Intel for the best place to land is just south of Sungmim. It would be about 3 km from the target area. There are many docks for container ships along the way. The port is very busy and well guarded. As you can see from their estimate, the docks themselves are not overly secured. That means that they have their main security folks busy checking vehicles entering and leaving the port. This will give you a big advantage if we can get to this area undetected."

Shree Webster raised her hand. Jon nodded for her to speak.

"Would it be possible to go into the port at Sungmim in a container ship from a Chinese company that normally ships goods to North Korea? That would reduce the chance of being detected. We could rig a container to accommodate our teams. We would have to figure out how to unload the container and get it moved to Sungmim. Maybe the Chinese MSS could handle that function." There was total silence in the room.

"Commander Webster that is a great idea. William and Dan, can you get in touch with the station chief in Shanghai and see if this is feasible?" said Jon.

"We'll get right on it", said Dan. They left the room to the little office down the hall.

"That is a fantastic idea, but will require a lot of prep work. I'll send Susan Daley an email to call me on this secure phone", said William. Dan pointed at the phone, "The number is printed on the base." William typed the short message to Susan Daley. He looked at his watch. It was coming up on 0600 in Shanghai. "Let's make a list of items we think will be required to make this work."

"Okay, here is one" said Dan. "Can a Chinese company be trusted to handle this?"

"Getting them to transport the container should be no problem. They don't have to know what's inside" said William.

"If the company could make arrangements with the North Korean port to expedite the transportation of the container to a location near the target on a priority basis, then the teams would be within a few blocks of the target totally undetected", said Dan.

The secure phone rang. William looked at his watch, 6:30 in Shanghai. "Hello this is William." He smiled. "Hi to you too. What are you doing up at this hour?" He listened for a moment. "We have an idea and need your help." William told Susan the idea of using a container from a well known Chinese company to get the team in and out of Sungmim. If the company could address the destination of the container to a few blocks from the target area and set a priority on the delivery it would be the best way to get the team in and out without detection. The pickup of the extraction team would have to be done within hours of delivery.

Susan expressed that she was impressed with the idea. She would speak to Jai Chun and get back to them.

Shanghai US Consulate, CIA office

Susan made notes and thought about how to make this idea happen. It was a brilliant scheme. She looked at her clock. It was 0715. She left her office and walked to the back of the empty office. Nu was at his desk typing on a computer. He looked up. "I didn't expect you to be here" said Nu. Susan smiled. "I have spoken to some of our assets in Beijing and confirmed that Madam Wo was away during the time Dr. Wu as kidnapped. No one seems to know where she was during the time in question. There is no doubt that she was here supervising the kidnapping", said Nu.

"Good work. I have something else that just came in. The extraction teams have a tentative plan. We need to get Jai's help with this one. It's big and time is against us." Susan explained the plan to Nu. He listened very carefully.

"I think that can be made to work. If the teams can configure the container in the States, load it on a C5 cargo plane and land it here in Shanghai, Jai will have to make the arrangements with a company to have the container picked up at the airport and taken to the ship. Then the shipping company will have to make arrangements to put a priority on the container's delivery and pickup. It's doable."

"Great. What would be a good cargo to use that would be accepted and with a priority?"

"Let me think about that. I will confer with my new team mate, Kow and get his input", said Nu.

"Good, I will ask Jai for a meeting this morning. How about 0900?"

"I'll be ready"

MSS Office Shanghai

Susan and Nu entered the MSS office and were immediately escorted to Jai Chun's conference room. When they arrived the same group that were present the day before were seated around the table. Jai welcomed Susan and Nu and motioned for them to be seated. "Ms. Daley since you requested this meeting, please proceed."

"Thank you. First we would like to share some Intel with you. Nu please up-date us on the kidnapping."

Nu stood. "I have received information that Madam Wo was unaccounted for during the time of Dr. Wu's kidnapping. We have DNA evidence that she was in fact in the safe house." Nu sat down.

"Thank you Mr. Lee. We too have been hard at work following up leads. It appears that the main North Korean crime family did indeed make a contract with the North Koreans to conduct the kidnapping of Dr. Wu's aunt. However, it appears they had nothing to do with the attack on your safe house. That was carried out by North Koreans. That supports what you have said about Madam Wo being in the safe house. She would not have been there with anyone except her own agents", said Jai Chun.

Susan stood. "I have come here to give you a briefing on a possible extraction plan. We need to run this by you to see if it is feasible. First, it is essential that the overall scope be examined carefully for flaws or possible failure." Susan gave the group a highlight of the plan. They all sat very attentive. "Now let's have questions and ideas."

Jai stood. "I will say that I think this is a workable plan. There are several companies that I can think of that will cooperate. There is one that imports meat from Australia. They will cooperate. Are there any questions or ideas?"

Mr. Kow stood. "Minister, let's assume we get a company to allow us to use them to ship and retrieve a container. What is to stop the North Korean's from opening the container and exposing our team? What cargo would be acceptable with minimum examination?"

Nu stood. "I have given this some thought. China exports a large amount of fresh meat to North Korea. This is done in refrigerated 12 meter containers. Naturally fresh meat would be given priority. We can construct a container to appear to contain a full load of fresh meat. We will also assure that the meat is well refrigerated. When and if the inspectors open the container, all they will see is rows of refrigerated meat. The construction of the container will be done in San Diego and brought here with the teams on a C5 cargo plane. The best estimate of construction will be 48 hours. The flight time here is 14.5 hours."

Jai looked at his crew. "Questions?"

A young man stood. "Mr. Lee, how will the extraction team get out of North Korea?"

"We have discussed this part of the plan. We need to know the normal turnaround time for these types of containers. We also need to know the customers of fresh meat and their locations. Do the customers have their own means of transporting the containers? If you can get to me the answers to these questions this afternoon, then we can begin the detail planning. The location of the customers is very important. Also if the containers are delivered around the clock, it would be great if our container could be delivered and picked up at night." Nu sat down.

"You are dismissed to get these questions answered", said Jai. "Kow you stay." The team left the conference room.

"Susan this is a workable solution. I want Kow and some of his team to be included in the extraction team." He looked from Susan to Nu for a reaction.

Susan looked at Jai with a wide smile. "I have told our people to expect your direct help with the extraction team. They are expecting you. We need to know how many so that the design of the crew space in the container is sufficient. I suggest speeding up our planning process, by limiting the meetings to the four of us plus anyone or two that Mr. Kow would like to include."

"Yes that is acceptable", said Jai. "Please feel free to work here until we find out the answers you need."

"Thank you, but we need to return to our teams and will be back at 1400", said Susan.

Shanghai US Consulate, CIA office

Susan and Nu returned to their office. Susan called the number William had sent earlier. William answered the phone.

"William, I have some information regarding the plan. It has been suggested that the cargo will be refrigerated fresh meat. The MSS are certain they have a company that imports meat from Australia that will cooperate with no questions asked. This afternoon we have another meeting to find out the details of how the shipping containers are handled and where the closest customer for fresh meat is located relative to the target."

"Wow, that's fast work. We are planning on flying back to the coast tomorrow. The team is being picked as we speak. One of yours came up with this idea; she is commander of the Blue Belt group. I am sure you will get to meet her."

"Thanks William, check your email later for details on the container handling." She pressed the disconnect button.

She went to Nu's cubical. He had left for lunch. She saw a note on his desk. There was a sum of money with a question mark and a note: *$3k. A contact may have a picture of Madam Wo with her agents leaving the safe house area.* Susan thought *that would certainly help Jai with his superiors.*

Chapter 23

Shanghai US Consulate, CIA offices

Susan sat staring at her computer screen showing a picture of Madam Wo. She was a middle aged woman with high cheek bones with a serious look. She would wait until Nu returned to question him on the mysterious note indicating evidence of Madam Wo being at the safe house.

An email notification popped up on her computer. It was from William. She put the email through the decryption program. It read there is a slight change in plans. *The container construction is going to take at least a week. The team is concerned about the Air Force plane landing in Shanghai with the container and the extraction team. They feel it is too much exposure. An updated plan is being processed and will be sent within six hours.* End of message.

Susan saw Nu going towards his cubical. She waited until he was seated and called his desk phone. "Nu, can you come to my office please?" She looked up and saw Nu coming towards her office. He came directly in and sat in the chair in front of her desk.

"I have been pressing my contacts in Beijing for information on the North Koreans spy agency in China. It appears I got a break. One of the contacts knows a private contractor for drone surveillance. He was hired by a North Korean crime family to have a drone follow the FBI car when it left the university. According to my contact there is a video showing Madam Wo arriving at the CIA safe house with several agents. They were inside for a short period of time. The video shows Madam Wo and Dr. Wu getting into a van and the agents who were with her left in a separate vehicle. The contractor wants Three Thousand US dollars to send the video."

"Nu if this video does show the kidnapping of Dr. Wu by Madam Wo, then we have a direct tie to the North Koreans. What do you have to do to get a copy of the video?"

"My contact says to wire the money to him and he will get the copy and email it to me. If he receives the money by noon, we should have a copy of the video within an hour.

Susan grabbed a blank voucher and filled it out for $3,000. She signed it and handed it to Nu. He nodded and left immediately for his cubical. He picked up a piece of paper with the banking information and nearly ran to the communication officer to wire the funds. He looked up at the clock. It was 1135 hours. He would meet the deadline. They should have the video before returning to the MSS offices.

MSS Office

Jai Chun had his two top agents in his office. They discussed the American's plan to extract Dr. Wu. The idea of the container was good with the exception of it being delivered on a US Air Force plane. There were too many eyes already in places they had no idea where.

"Sir, what if the American's delivered the container and the extraction team to Australia. No one would give it a second thought. The container can be added to the bunch leaving the meat works each week."

Jai looked pleased. This would solve one of his greatest fears. If the extraction team was exposed, the North Koreans may dispose of Dr. Wu to save face. "Good work. I agree the plan has a major problem of remaining secret if the American's land their Air Force plane on Chinese soil. I am meeting with the Americans in a few hours. I will bring this up." The agents left Jai's office. Jai knew that if the extraction team and the container were delivered to Australia, it would take at least a week for the container to arrive in Shanghai. They would have to live with that.

Shanghai US Consulate, CIA office

Nu ate lunch at his desk. He was nervous about the contact actually following through with the video. He knew the contact would have to steal the video. That added a layer of uncertainty. It was possible he was being played. The contact had delivered information previously but only verbal information. This was different. He kept looking at his email for any new arrivals—Nothing. The time on his monitor showed 1315. They would have to leave for the MSS meeting in thirty minutes. This was cutting it close. A beep brought his attention to focus on his screen. There it was with an MP4 attachment of 1.4 GB. He downloaded the video to his hard drive and also to a thumb drive.

Nu double clicked the MP4 file. The video displayed on the screen. At first it showed a black SUV moving toward a normal looking home in the suburbs. He could clearly see a man get out of the car and go into the house. He returned and opened the door for another man and a woman wearing a hat and sweat shirt. It was not clear if this was Dr. Wu.

The video switched scenes to the couple leaving by another car and going into what appeared to be an abandoned residential area. The car stopped and a man got out and went into a rundown house. The man returned. The video close up clearly showed that it was in fact Dr. Wu. She and a man got out of the SUV and went into the house. The picture then switched to a car approaching. A woman got out and went into the house. It was Susan Daley.

The man who had accompanied Dr. Wu came out and got into the car and left. A few minutes later, Susan Daley left the house.

The scene switched to a van driving up and four men and a woman getting out and running into the house. The angle showing the woman did not show her face.

The scene switched again and showed Dr. Wu, a man and the woman coming out of the door approaching another van. This time there was no mistake, the picture was very clear; this was Madam Wo and Dr. Wu leaving the safe house. As soon as the van left the scene, three more men came out of the house. They did not seem to be in a hurry. They drove away in the same direction as Madam Wo and Dr. Wu.

Nu clapped his hands and stuck the USB drive into his pocket and headed for Susan's office. He tapped lightly and went in. Susan looked up and she saw him holding the USB drive.

"Is that the video?" asked Susan.

"Yes and it is more than I hoped for." He handed the drive to Susan. She inserted it into her computer. The video played through without any comments from her or Nu.

Susan sat back. "Wow, oh wow. This is going to blow Jai's mind. He has evidence to arrest Madam Wo. This will tie the kidnapping and murder of our men to North Korea, if Jai has solid evidence that Madam Wo is in fact the head of the North Korean spy group in China." She looked at the clock. "We have to go." She removed the USB drive and handed it to Nu and they walked to the car park for the short ride to the MSS office.

MSS Office

When Susan and Nu entered the conference room, they noticed there were only four people. Jai, Kow and two agents who were in the earlier meetings.

"Jai, gentlemen, we have something that I think will make your day, your week and maybe your year." She nodded to Nu. He reached into his pocket and handed her the USB drive. She handed it to Jai who put it into a computer on the table.

The video played through. There was dead silence in the room. Jai grinned and slapped his hand on the table. "People, this is the kind of intelligence we need from our agents. Susan this is more than I expected."

"Thank Nu, he and his contacts came up with this. It clearly indicates that Madam Wo was involved in the kidnapping of Dr. Wu and the murder of my men. This does little to get Dr. Wu back or provide any revenge for the murder of our agents."

"Yes, you are correct. We must concentrate on getting Dr. Wu back. We will arrest Madam Wo in due time. We will be watching her every move. He sat down and turned off the computer. "We have discussed the extraction plan and feel there is a major security risk in the team and the container being delivered here in a US Air Force plane. We have another suggestion." He looked at Susan.

"I too have some concerns about the plan. I got an email from the FBI that they have a modification to the plan, but have not sent the details as of yet. What are your suggestions?"

"We discussed the possibility of the container and team to fly directly to Australia and the container be put with the normal cargo leaving Townsville. I know the team would be required to stay in the container for over a week or longer but we feel it is the only safe option. Once the container reaches Shanghai, our three members can join your team and then be transported to North Korea."

"Jai, I will pass on your concerns and plan as soon as I get back to the office. I personally think you are right. If the technical issue with the team being in the container for over a week doesn't complicate the plan, then I think it's a go. I might suggest that the container be set aside in a secure place to give the team a chance to stretch their legs and meet your three members."

"Yes, I agree. The container can be separated from the others in a secure location and your team can disembark. The trip to North Korea on a container vessel is about three days."

"Have you found any answers to our questions about customers near the target and the normal turn-around for the container? Also, can the container be delivered at night and picked up at night?"

Jai motioned for Kow to speak. "The nearest customer is two blocks away. It is a state run hotel for high ranking members. Also, the transport company delivers twenty four hours per day. We can make arrangements for the container to be delivered after midnight and picked up before dawn."

"That is great. When we get Dr. Wu back to Shanghai, what are the procedures for taking her back to the USA?"

"Jai hesitated. We have not addressed that part of the plan. I must speak to my superiors on the proper way to handle this issue. I personally don't think we will need more than a video statement from Dr. Wu and allowing for any need for the prosecuting attorney to question both Dr. Wu and her aunt, Mrs. Wang, I should think she will be ready to leave within two days of arrival in Shanghai."

"That sounds good for me. We would like to take Mrs. Wang with us. Can arrangements be made for a passport and exit visa?"

"Leave that with me, I will personally see that all paper work is complete."

The meeting broke up and Susan and Nu returned to the CIA office. Susan called William directly.

Shanghai US Consulate, CIA office

"William good morning. Sorry if I woke you, but we have a suggestion for the extraction plan."

"No problem Susan", he said with a yawn.

"The team here suggests that the container and team be flown to Townsville, Queensland, Australia instead of Shanghai. The company chosen by the MSS has a meat works in western Queensland. Our container can be added to the shipment out of Townsville without a problem. The MSS have three agents they want included in the team. The transit time from Townsville to Shanghai is one week. Arrangements must be made for the team to be inside the container for at least seven to ten days."

"Wow, that's a long time to be cooped up in a container. The team is six, one female and five males plus your three. I will get back to you. Time is against us. I really don't see how we can get into the target zone before three to four weeks. Everyone must agree to this long delay."

"Okay, I will wait to hear back from you before I talk with the MSS again." They terminated the call. Susan was not happy with the extraction being delayed for up to two and maybe three weeks. A lot can happen in that time span.

Chapter 24

North Korean lab

Li Ming studied the results of the last test on the power supply. The input voltage had been smoothed out and the power supply was delivering a steady stream of ions. It had been nearly three weeks since her arrival and without a day off.

Dauen was a great help. The parts she ordered were perfect. Li Ming knew that the safety of Dauen's family was constantly on her mind. She wasn't eating properly and cried nearly every night. Li Ming decided it was time to contact her aunt again. She was curious as to what kind of message she would send this time.

Kwang was seated in the little conference room. Li Ming walked in and took a seat. "I need to speak to my aunt. If any harm has come to her, you will never get the device to work."

Kwang sat and stared at Li Ming. He nodded and opened the drawer containing the satellite phone. He pressed the recall button and held the phone to his ear. "Let me speak to the old woman." He waited nearly a minute before he heard her voice. "Have you been treated fairly?" He listened for a few seconds. "Your niece is here and wants to speak to you." He passed the phone to Li Ming.

"Aunt, are you OK?" She listened to her aunt tell her how she had been treated. "I see, and are you eating okay?"

"Yes, I don't like the Korean food. How long does it take to bake your recipe for spice cakes?"

Li Ming knew she was asking a question about time but what time. Then it hit her, how much time before the device is functional. "Aunt it takes about four hours to completely bake."

Kwang reached and took the phone. "Put my man back on the phone." He waited for the man to answer. "I want a daily report on her condition. I will call you each morning." He pressed the end button and replaced the phone in the drawer.

Kwang studied Li Ming for a moment. How long before you connect the power supply and test the device?"

"The power supply test should be completed today. I am very tired. The next phase is critical and I'm not sure I'm up to performing the calibration test as tired as I am. I need a day or two off."

Kwang screwed up his face. "Maybe after the test you can have a day off."

"You are taking a very big chance. If I miss-calibrate the ion flow, the device will be damaged and will take a month to repair."

"If you damage the device then your aunt will not fair so well. Do I make myself clear?"

"If anything should happen to my aunt your program will end. You can do anything you want with me, but my aunt cannot be touched." She got up and left the room.

CIA Special Apartment

The agent closed the sat phone. The recording of the conversation was immediately sent to Susan's office. She heard the ding of the arriving message with the attachment. She opened the message and clicked on the attachment and listened to the conversation. Li Ming had said four hours. That could mean four days or four weeks. She had to make sure which.

The next morning at 0815 the sat phone rang. The agent clicked the icon on the computer connected to the phone. He answered. "She refuses to eat. I have tried everything. She wants to speak to her niece."

Kwang frowned and sent one of the guards to get Li Ming. "Why does she not eat?"

The agent was careful with his answer. "She says she is worried about her niece."

"I see. Well here she is. Put the woman on the phone." Kwang heard the old woman's voice and handed the phone to Li Ming.

"Aunt, are you safe and okay?" She listened to the response.

"Li Ming, I am so worried. The shop is closed and they say I can't go and check on it. I know I ordered books before they took me away. How long does it take for the books to arrive?"

North Korean lab

Li Ming thought, she is asking how many weeks before the device is ready. "Aunt, if all goes well it takes about four weeks, sometimes longer."

Kwang reached and took the phone. "Have you been treated fairly?"

"Yes, they treat me well. The food is not to my liking and I can't eat most of it. I don't like Korean food. It is too spicy."

"Put my man back on the phone."

"Yes sir."

"I want you to get Chinese food for her. Ask her what she wants and get it for her." He pressed the end button without any further conversation.

Li Ming returned to her work bench. Dauen was very nervous. She dropped a pair of calibration forks. Li Ming bent over to pick them up. Dauen was bent over too. She whispered "They told me we would have to work every day until the device was tested."

Li Ming winked at Dauen. They continued to test the power supply. At 1600 hours, the power supply had completed its test successfully.

Li Ming went to the conference room and told Kwang that the power supply was ready to be integrated with the device. She was very concerned about her focus and concentration needed for the integration test. Could she have at least one day off to rest?

Jung was seated at the table. She stared at Li Ming. "You have done well to catch up the time schedule. You may have tomorrow off. Then I want that device up and working."

"Thank you. I will do my best." Li Ming left the room smiling. She walked up to the bench and winked at Dauen.

"What did they say about the test?" asked Dauen.

"They said we had done a good job of catching up the schedule and we can have tomorrow off." Dauen smiled and for the first time in days she had positive look about her. Li Ming was pleased.

Shanghai US Consulate, CIA office

Susan listened to the latest recording. There was no mistaking the reference to four weeks and maybe longer. So the device would be ready maybe in four weeks. At least they had a timetable. She sent off an email with the timetable to William. She had not heard back about the new suggestion for the extraction plan.

Nu and Kow reported on the logistics of getting the container to a secure location. It seemed the port itself was the best. If the team wore Chinese uniforms, they would be less likely to be discovered. Nu made arrangements for the uniforms to be sent to Townsville, Queensland.

Camp Pendleton, California

The extraction team sat in the conference room discussing the plan. Dan and William passed on the suggestion from Susan Daley. They liked the security of the plan but were concerned about the length of time required for the team to be locked in the container.

Jon clapped his hands. The room went silent. "People, it seems we have only four weeks to get this mission completed. The configuration of the container is going well. They will complete the modifications in six days. The engineers tell me the crew quarters will accommodate ten people for up to three weeks. That is the good news. The bad news is three of the MSS agents will be added once you reach Shanghai. We have no Intel on these men and what their qualifications are."

Shree Webster raised her hand. Jon nodded. "Fellow commanders, I suggest we ask the MSS to send their three agents to Australia to train with us. We can leave tomorrow and it will give us almost seven days to get to know them and integrate them into our team."

The room was silent. Every eye was focused on Shree. Jon cleared his throat. "Commander Webster, I like that suggestion. It gives us breathing room to absorb the Chinese into our team. Doing that in

Shanghai with only a day or two is not good. William, you and Dan contact Susan Daley and inform her of this suggestion and get an answer back by 1800 hours."

William and Dan left the room. Jon looked each commander in the eye. "This is going to be a very high profile extraction. I want a final assignment list by 1800. I will make arrangements for you to leave before noon tomorrow. Don't worry about the construction of the container—I will personally see that it meets all of our expectations. Now I suggest you work on the final team roster and meet back here at 1800, dismissed."

Jon tapped Shree Webster on the shoulder to wait. Once the two were alone, Jon asked her to be seated. "Commander, the conditions related to living in the container for a week or longer may be extremely uncomfortable. Having to live in such close quarters with men may not be a good idea under normal circumstances. With the tension of the mission and the confining conditions, I'm asking you to reconsider your position with the group."

Shree sat still. She had been expecting something like this to come up. "Sir, I have been in the Middle East for over two years. I have had to endure some unimaginable conditions. Being locked up with a bunch of men for a week or so is something I can handle."

Jon got up and paced to the back of the room and back. "I know you are a very seasoned combat commander. I know you have a skill we need on this mission. I just want you to be sure you feel comfortable with these conditions." Jon sat down.

"I'm very comfortable with the mission."

Nothing more was said. Jon nodded and they left the room.

***

Dan and William used a major's office to call Susan Daley. Susan was in the process of closing up her office and going upstairs to her apartment when her secure phone rang.

"Susan, this is William. The mission is a go with the team leaving for Australia tomorrow. The team would like to have the three MSS agents meet them in Australia for training. It will give them time to adjust to each other and develop a strategic plan for the extraction."

"That's a great plan. I will contact Jai immediately and make the arrangements. Where in Australia should they meet?"

"We are suggesting commercial flights to Townsville, Queensland. There is a large Air Force base in Townsville. We will make arrangements to let us use their facilities for a training exercise. The configured container will be flown directly to Townsville. Arrangements will be made for the cargo to be delivered from the meat plant to Townsville and put into our container. Our container will then join all the others at the Townsville port for transport to Shanghai."

"I'll call you back in ten minutes." Susan immediately called Jai. He answered on the first ring. She explained the plan.

"I agree. It makes sense to have the team train as much as possible together. Where in Australia are they going to train?"

"Townsville, it is north of Brisbane. I suggest your men pose as textile business men. They can take the uniforms as samples of their work. Have them take a flight from Hong Kong to Brisbane and then to Townsville. Our team will be in place late tomorrow. As soon as your team arrives in Brisbane, they should call our team and make connection arrangements. I will have the phone number and contact name first thing in the morning."

"That sounds like a good plan. I will be expecting your call." Jai hung up.

Susan was pleased the plan went well. She called William. He answered immediately. "William, it's a go. The three men will be posing as textile business men. They will have uniforms for the team. We have changed from Chinese to North Korean army uniforms. I need sizes and a phone number and name for them to contact when they clear customs in Brisbane. Is the team traveling commercial?"

"That has not been determined yet. The General is making arrangements with the Australians for the use of their facilities in Townsville. As soon as the details are completed, I'll send you an email. It should not be more than a few hours from now."

"Great, I'll keep you informed on any developments here." She did not mention the video of Madam Wo. It seemed best that if it is revealed it should come from Jai. She closed her office door and headed to the elevator. She saw Nu in his cubical. She thought, *that guy is a gift.*

Chapter 25

North Korea

Li Ming and Dauen had the day off and slept half of it. They both felt refreshed. They ate the midday meal and decided to go shopping for food items. Dauen went to the door and asked the guard if they could go shopping. "I will check and let you know", said the guard.

A few minutes later there was a soft knock on the door. Dauen answered the door. The man in the suit was with the guard. "Why do you want to go shopping?"

"We would like to get some food supplies. It will help relax us."

The man thought for a moment. "I will give you two hours, no more. Be ready to leave in ten minutes."

"Thank you. We will be ready to go." Dauen was excited and told Li Ming to get ready to go shopping. Li Ming smiled and hurried to get dressed. She slipped her iPhone into a pocket. She was not sure it was compatible with the North Korean cell system, but it was worth a try. They heard the knock on the door and the man in the suit and the guard escorted them to the car. The drive to the shopping area was short.

The man got out of the car and waited until they climbed out. "I will be going with you. Please do not try anything foolish."

They walked through the long passage with vendors on each side. When they walked into the center square, there were lots of women with children playing in the small playground. There were only a few men in the square. Li Ming saw a butcher shop across the park area. She pointed at the shop and grabbed Dauen's hand. She led Dauen across the square. The suit followed.

The shop was full of different meats. Li Ming chose a chicken and a pork roast. She then remembered she had no money. "Dauen do you have any money? I forgot I have none." Dauen looked through her purse and found only a few notes. "Not nearly enough to pay for the food."

The man she called the suit was watching them hunt for money. The suit stepped in and paid for the goods. While he was paying the bill, Li Ming sneaked her phone out. There was a signal. She carefully replaced the phone. The suit turned and looked at Li Ming. At first she thought he had seen her looking at her phone. "We go now", said the suit.

They returned to the apartment.

North Korea lab

The next day, testing the power supply was complete. It was stable and the ion flow was within the proper range. Li Ming began the tedious calibrations. Dauen watched with awe. She had never seen such perfection.

"Hold the calibration fork on this terminal", said Li Ming.

Dauen moved the fork over to the indicated terminal. "How can we tell if the flow is being accepted", said Dauen.

"We can't just yet. We have to couple the power supply to the wave exciter stage. That will take about three or four days. The coupling is very sensitive and is polarized. It must be done very slowly and at the lowest possible setting." Li Ming explained that the wave exciter is the main producer of the phase field. "If the wave exciter comes online too fast the field will collapse and could be badly damaged. A new yoke coil would have to be manufactured. That would take a week so we have to be very careful."

Late in the afternoon, the first test was complete and the field did not collapse. Kwang watched as they tidied up the work area. He motioned for the guard to bring Dauen to the conference room.

The guard approached the two women. He told Dauen that Kwang wanted to speak to her. Dauen told Li Ming that Kwang wanted to speak to her. Li Ming raised an eyebrow. This was the first time Dauen had been summoned by Kwang. She followed the guard to the conference room.

Kwang was seated as was Jung. "Please have a seat Dauen", said Kwang. "We want a report on the progress." Dauen was shocked they were asking her. Why not ask Li Ming?

"The first test of the integration was completed today. The field held and the ion flow was within bounds. Li Ming says that within in three or four more days we should be ready to test the first stage of the device."

Rhee Sung-min leaned forward and looked directly into Dauen's eyes. "Do you think Li Ming is holding back on testing?"

"No, she is going as fast as possible. If the ion flow is too great it will damage the wave exciter and the yoke coil will have to be rebuilt. That would take one or two weeks. She is very careful and that takes time."

"I see. So you feel she is going as fast as possible?"

"Yes. We hope to get at least ten percent of the startup by tomorrow."

Kwang looked at Jung. She nodded. "You may go", said Kwang.

Dauen returned to the work area and finished helping Li Ming to put all the equipment away. No one spoke. The guard escorted them to the waiting car.

No one spoke on the way to the apartment building. Once in the apartment, Li Ming went to the bathroom and took out her iPhone. There was no signal. She wrote on a pad.

iPhone works in the shopping area but not here. We will have to go back to the shopping area to call your sister, maybe in a week or so.

She removed the page and folded it carefully into a small square and returned to the lounge. Dauen had turned on the TV to the music station.

Li Ming walked into the room. "Hi, what's on the TV?"

"I turned on music, but if you want something else we can change the station."

"No that is fine. I want to read a little so the music is fine. I might turn it down a bit." She reached for the remote and turned down the volume. When she put the remote down she placed the small square of paper under the remote. Dauen saw the note but looked away. They knew they were being watched.

Li Ming went to her room and got the book she was reading. It was an old novel, but at least it was something to take her mind off the lab. When she returned to the lounge she noticed the paper under the remote was gone. Dauen was in her bathroom.

Dauen came back to the lounge and sat on the sofa. She watched the TV. After a few minutes she looked over at Li Ming who was reading. "What do you want for the evening meal?"

Li Ming looked up. "Let's try a dish I really like. It's called General Cho's chicken. I can fix it. You fix fried rice and I will cook the chicken."

Dauen had a wide grin. "I have heard of General Cho's chicken but never tasted it. Is it hard to fix?"

"No. Why don't you take notes and when you return home, you can fix it for your family. The sauce is the key."

Li Ming went back to her book. Dauen continued to watch the TV orchestra.

There was a knock on the door. They looked at each other. Dauen went to the door. Suit was standing in the hall with the guard. "You will prepare enough food for us too." He watched her expression. She smiled and said it would be her pleasure. She saw the Suit and the guard smile for the first time. She closed the door. Li Ming was watching but had no idea what was said.

Dauen came in and sat down. "They want us to fix enough food for them also." Li Ming looked puzzled. "I think they must be hungry for General Cho's chicken." They both laughed. She was not sure the watchers and listeners understood Chinese, but they understood General Cho's chicken.

They both were busy chopping and stirring. The chicken was browned and the sauce was bubbling in a small pot. Li Ming watched as Dauen wrote the phone number for her sister on the note pad. The watchers would think she was taking notes. The rice was done and the sauce had been poured over the fried chicken.

Dauen went to the door and suit and the guard were already standing waiting for the door to open. Dauen welcomed them into the apartment.

As strange as it seemed, the four ate and laughed and enjoyed the evening meal. The Suit and the guard left and the apartment was back to normal. Dauen gathered up the dishes and they both washed and dried.

Dauen had left the phone number on the note pad lying on the coffee table. Li Ming saw the page with the number. She made no attempt to get it. After the music program completed, they decided it was bed time. Li Ming closed her book and Dauen picked up her note pad. "Li Ming, look over my notes and make sure it is correct. I loved General Cho's chicken." Li Ming picked up the note pad and went to her bedroom. She put the note pad on the bedside table and went into the bathroom to dress for sleep.

The next morning Li Ming took the note pad into the bathroom and put the number into her phone. Then she flushed the page down the toilet. She hid her iPhone in a waterproof plastic bag in the toilet tank. She was certain they searched their room each day. With the lights out, she had tested with a string pasted across a drawer opening on the dresser. Each day when she returned the string had been disturbed.

The laundry was done by someone unknown. She was told to leave her items to be washed in the basket provided. She was grateful for the laundry service. She was thinking how to get Kwang to let them have another day off. She would tell the man in the suit she had to use the bathroom while at the shopping mall. It would give her privacy to phone Dauen's sister. But then she remembered, she did not speak Korean. Change of plans. Dauen would use the phone. She had to teach Dauen how to use her iPhone.

Chapter 26

Townsville, Queensland, Australia

The large private jet landed and taxied to a remote hanger. The extraction team and William Braun quickly deplaned and went into the hanger. It was early in the morning. The flight from Honolulu had taken almost eight hours.

Jon motioned for all of the team to gather around. "People, this is the first phase of the plan. I know most did not sleep well on the trip, but we must be ready for training. As we discussed, we will do all of our training in the evening. This will give us a realistic platform and also avoid any curious watchers. Get some rest and be ready by 1800 hours."

Two uniformed Australian soldiers escorted the team to accommodations. The rooms were neat and had all of the amenities of a good motel.

Jon and William were introduced to Kow and two of his team. They arrived two hours earlier from Brisbane. Kow spoke English but with a struggle. The other two were almost fluent. That would help with communications. "Gentlemen, I am Jon Ferguson. I am the leader of the extraction team. Welcome. We will be training each evening until we get orders to move to Shanghai. Be here at 1800 hours to meet your team mates."

Kow nodded and motioned for his two team members to follow the Australian soldier, who had been waiting a few feet away, to the living area.

William told Jon he had to check-in. "I'm going to attempt to get a few hours sleep" said Jon. He saw the Australian soldier coming from the living area and waved to be led to his room.

William called Susan Daley. "Hi William. I hope you had a smooth flight."

"It was okay. The MSS trio showed up. We will begin training this evening. The container is due here in three days. As soon as it is in place and we check everything out and will be ready to go."

"That's great" said Susan. "There have not been any new developments. We are expecting to get the details on merging the container into the shipment from the meat packing plant in the next few days. Dr. Wu's aunt is fine and staying with our special unit. She has spoken with Dr. Wu three times. We think the device will be ready in three weeks. That is cutting it close, but if we can extract Dr. Wu before it is completed, that will stop the North Koreans from planting the WMD's in mainland China."

"I will check in each morning. Thanks for the update", said William. He pressed the end key and terminated the call.

Susan thought *Three weeks, wow, and such a short time. The world as we know it may change dynamically and for the worse.*

North Korea High Command

Seok Dong-Suk sat very still. He was hoping the General would not call on him for a report. He had really nothing to report. The meeting was not going well. Most of the military leaders were actually followers. They did whatever the general wanted done.

The general made it clear they were going ahead with the plan to place nuclear devices in specific places in China. He asked the female scientist in charge of producing the war heads if they were on schedule. The scientist stood and bowed. "Yes sir. Seven war heads have been completed. The eighth is being assembled and will be ready in two days." The general nodded his approval.

The general turned to Seok Dong-Suk. "What can you report to us on the readiness of the transport device?"

Seok Dong-Suk nearly jumped when the general asked him to report. He looked up and saw the general scowling at him as if he had done something unpleasant. "Sir, the device's power supply has been completed and tested. The integration to the device is being done now. Because of the sensitive nature of the procedure it is estimated the device will be ready for testing in three weeks."

The general stared at the center of the table. "It had better be ready in three weeks. We are a month behind and the Chairman is not happy." With that he turned and left the room.

Seok Dong-Suk felt like he had been beaten with a bat. He knew the military leadership was on thin ice with the Chairman. If they did not produce something before the Chairman had talks with the Western powers in five weeks, then most of the leadership would be replaced. His asset in Beijing was providing the intelligence as to where to place the WMD's. Her last communication indicated that the specific locations had to be vetted personally before she could confirm the list and he could expect to have the list in a few days.

The attendees filed out of the room. Most were not going to be involved in the mission. Some were secretly hoping for a failure. Their future careers would be secure if the mission did not happen.

MSS office Shanghai

Jai Chun sat in his office thinking. *The Americans have enough evidence for an arrest. But I prefer to get my own hard evidence and make a public event of the arrest.*

Jai made a call to Beijing. His number one agent had been left in charge while he was away in Shanghai. He instructed him to put a twenty-four seven watch on Madam Wo. He wanted video, audio and photos of her every contact. Jai instructed him to put as many men as necessary to assure every move she made was recorded.

As soon as he hung up from the Beijing call his cell phone rang. It was his wife. She had received an invitation to a play from Madam Wo. She wanted to know if Jai would be back in time to attend. Jai immediately said yes. He was coming back tomorrow. "When is the play?" She told him it was in two days, on Wednesday. Jai smiled and said his goodbye and hung up.

He was thinking. *So she is going about business as usual. Maybe this is going to be harder than I thought. How to separate her social life from her spy life was not going to be easy. She hob knobbed with all the elite in Beijing including the political bunch. Anyone could be a traitor.*

Jai got up from his desk and walked around the huge central room.

He missed Kow. He was very good at his craft. He looked into Kow's office and was surprised to see Nu typing on a computer keyboard. "Nu what are you doing here?"

"Sir, I am following up on a lead. It appears that Madam Wo is producing a play that will be going around to some of the major cities during the next three weeks. Personally I think she is using this as an elaborate cover. It may be to sort out some locations for the nuclear devices. It would be an ideal way to do this without any suspicion."

Jai sat down in the chair in front of Nu. "Well that makes sense. I have ordered her watched and recorded. If she is looking for places to place the devices, then we will record every move she makes."

"Sir, do we have any idea how large these nuclear devices are?"

"I am told that if they are the same as tthe ones flashed all over the world press, then they are considerably heavy due to shielding. I am still skeptical of Dr. Wu's device being able to deliver these things."

"From what information I have been told about the capabilities of the transport device, there is almost no limit to size or weight. It was reported that one of the experiments transported an entire ship from Philadelphia to Norfolk and back." He saw Jai's eyes bulge out. Sweat started to appear on his forehead.

"That has to be some unfounded rumor. A ship? Not possible."

Nu said nothing more. Jai got up with a worried look on his face. His mind was going in flashes. *Should I tell the President? Maybe I should wait until more information comes in. Surely someone will have answers that contradict these absurd speculations. A young woman cannot build such a device.*

Chapter 27

North Korean lab

Li Ming was sure the ion stream was perfect. She and Dauen were assembling the yoke coil when several people came into the lab. They were unknown to Li Ming.

Kwang came in and introduced the four men and one woman as scientists who would be observing the integration process. The woman stepped forward. "My name is Min Chang. I am the lead scientist on this project. Please explain the procedure."

Li Ming just stood and stared at the woman. Finally she pointed at the power supply. She explained the yoke coil was extremely fragile and needed to be assembled in two stages.

Min Chang nodded she understood. The four men examined the power supply. "Li Ming, why is the device not ready?"

"I have no idea how to produce a test without first making sure all the parts are functioning."

"And, how are you going to make sure all the parts are functioning without a test."

"Once we have the yoke assembled and slowly bring up the ion flow then we will be ready for a small test of the systems. This will not allow for any transfer but just to make sure all the fields and beams are aligned."

"And how long will it take to run the test?" said Min Chang.

"The first phase should not take but a few days maybe a week. The second phase maybe two weeks."

"Well, we are here to help speed up things. Please carry on and we will observe the assembly."

Li Ming turned back to the work bench and motioned for Dauen to continue the assembly of the yoke coil. The small group of scientists surrounded the bench. For the next three hours, Li Ming carefully moved the yoke into position and began to attach the sensors. This was the critical part of the assembly. She did not like having all these people looking over her shoulder. The sensors were in place and Dauen began to bring up the ion beam from the power supply. The oscilloscope began to show waves and squiggly lines. "Shut it down", said Li Ming. "The beam is not aligned correctly." Min Chang stepped up and demanded an explanation.

Li Ming busily adjusted several controls and measured the beam. "I'm sorry, but you are distracting me. Please stand away from the bench until we get the yoke aligned." Min Chang didn't move. The other four moved back from the bench. Li Ming turned to the woman. "Please move back and give us room to work."

Min Chang stared at Li Ming but didn't move. "Okay, if that is the way you want to play this, I'm done" said Li Ming. She powered off the systems and began to pack up her tools.

Min Chang stomped over to the small conference room where Kwang was working. "This woman is not cooperating. Please lock her up and teach her who is in charge here."

Kwang sat very still. This was not how to get the device to work. He picked up his phone and called Jung. "I think you should come to the lab immediately. We have a problem." He hung up the phone. "You will have your answer in a few minutes." He ignored Min Chang and went back working on a report.

The door to the lab swung open. An armed guard and Jung came into the room. She looked over at the work bench and saw several people gathered around Li Ming and Dauen. She went to Kwang's office. She was surprised to see Min Chang. She knew of her and her work. She was not a fan but understood her power. "Min Chang, I'm happy to see you. What do we owe the visit?"

Chang smiled. "It seems your captured lab technician is not cooperating. She refuses to allow us full access to the device. She was insubordinate and needs to be taught a lesson."

"First, she is not a lab technician. She is the designer and inventor of the device. She is under my care and is on schedule after fixing some of our mistakes. Now if you don't mind, please have your people leave these facilities."

Min Chang was furious. "You have over stepped your authority with me. We shall see who is in charge here." She left the office and waved for her group to follow her.

Kwang smiled. "Well, she sure is a piece of work. I wonder what she is going to do. Maybe bring back a squad of soldiers and take over the building?"

Jung was not amused. "Be prepared to be ordered to step down and let her have her way. I'm very concerned about Li Ming. If she stops work, then they will most likely torture her. From what I have observed, that will be a waste of time. I don't think we should reveal we have Li Ming's aunt in captivity. Bring Li Ming in here and let's have a talk."

Kwang got up and went into the lab. Li Ming and Dauen were closing up the doors on the cupboards containing the test equipment. "We need to talk. Please follow me." Li Ming looked at Dauen and winked. She fell in behind Kwang as they walked to his office.

Jung was standing. She motioned for Li Ming to have a seat at the conference table. "Li Ming, I'm sure you were irritated by the attitude of Min Chang. She is a very powerful scientist in charge of North Korea's nuclear program. She is accustomed to being in charge. She is very ruthless and will stop at nothing to get her way. Do I make myself clear?"

"Yes, I understand. Min Chang does not realize there are critical steps that must be taken before the device can be activated. If we do not have all the components aligned perfectly, the device will malfunction and may be badly damaged."

"Yes, we understand that. You may not have an opportunity to properly do the alignment. Do what she wants and be sure to document everything she orders you to do. We think we will be ordered to turn over the project to her. I'm sorry. I know you have worked very hard to meet our schedule. Please don't do anything that will jeopardize your safety."

Li Ming was not expecting this from Jung. "Thank you for your encouragement. I will do what is asked even if it risks the success of the device. Please let me speak to my aunt one more time. I'm not sure what will happen to me."

Jung nodded at Kwang. He opened the drawer and removed the satellite phone. He waited for an answer. Finally he heard the man answer."Put the old woman on the phone." It took about a minute for her to come to the phone.

"Hello, Li Ming is that you?"

"Yes aunt. Everything is fine. Are you being cared for properly?"

"Yes, they bring me Chinese food now. The book order has not arrived. How long should it take?"

"I don't know, maybe two more weeks maybe less. The company is now different than when we ordered, so be prepared for the order to come any day." Kwang reached for the phone.

"Thank you put my man back on the line."

"Yes sir", said the man.

"I want you to be very good to her. If anyone other than me calls, hang up. Do not speak to anyone other than me. Is that clear?"

"Yes sir, only you." The line went dead.

Shanghai US Consulate, CIA office

Susan's computer dinged. She noted that a recording of the latest phone call to Li Ming's aunt had been delivered. She listened carefully. She got the message. Li Ming is now under some other authority. It appears things are speeding up. Kwang is not happy with a change of the guard. He does not want his people to be part of the new group. Not good.

Susan picked up her phone and punched in the number of Jai Chun. He answered on the second ring. "Jai, this is Susan. Is this a good time?"

"Yes, I am packing for my trip back to Beijing."

"We received a call from the lab in North Korea. Li Ming spoke to her aunt. There seems to be a change in the authority over the device. It appears they may speed things up. That will mean someone at the top is now pushing for the device to work. Madam Wo will be asked to make the decisions on the locations faster.

"Hum, that is not good. We think she is producing a play and taking it on the road as a front to pick the locations. I am going to the play on Wednesday in Beijing. The extraction team should be ready to go by next Monday. Kow is very impressed with their capabilities."

"Thanks Jai. Have a safe trip and enjoy the play."

Susan consulted a small book and punched in a number."William, Susan here. How are things shaping up?"

"Everything is on schedule. The container will arrive tomorrow and the team will begin to outfit it for the trip. The Chinese three are very good. They fitted right in. Jon told me they are better than expected."

"That's good. Look we may have a problem. It appears the North Koreans are moving up their schedule. It may happen within the next two weeks. That's cutting it close for you to get in and get out. If any more Intel comes in on their schedule, I'll phone you."

"Thanks Susan. Talk soon." The connection terminated. William knew there was nothing to be done to speed up the extraction. They were now locked into the shipping schedule for the meat works.

Cal Tech lab

Dr. March stood in front of a screen where a schematic diagram was projected. "People, we have reconstructed all but one piece of software for the device. It seems Li Ming kept that to herself. We have tested the device with limited success. We can send matter but not retrieve it. I want all of you to concentrate on this problem. Time is of the essence." He looked into the faces of the young group of scientists and hoped they would succeed. The CIA was pressing him for a working device. He was not sure why. It appeared they have some very secret purpose.

Chapter 28

Townsville, Queensland, Australia

William received a call while in the lunch hall. He got up and walked to a far corner. "Yes, I understand. We have completed the testing of the air system and the hygiene systems. All work perfectly. We are ready. Let us know the shipping schedule and we will be on our way." He terminated the call from Washington. He felt good about the Lotus Project.

Jon Ferguson pushed his men hard. They were ready. The three Chinese were just what he needed to make the team whole. They had provided the skills his men did not have. They spoke the languages and looked the part. He knew if contact was made these three would be the tip of the spear. He trusted them.

The container was a work of art. Thirty two feet of a forty foot container had been transformed into a living quarters for Jon's team. The walls were twelve inches thick with insulation to keep weather and sound from penetrating. The refrigeration equipment on the front of the container had been redesigned to also provide power for lighting and communications. The intake for the environmental system was designed to look like a normal vent for the generator. Backup batteries were concealed in the back wall in the event the generator malfunctioned.

The sleeping area was designed to give privacy and at the same time provide comfortable bedding with three bunks stacked. The food prep area was a marvel. There was storage for three weeks of food and water. A microwave and infrared oven would provide for cooking meals.

The ventilation system was copied from the International Space Station with the exception that there was an intake for outside air. All the air was scrubbed in special devices to remove CO_2 and replace with Oxygen. The eating area was also designed to provide entertainment with videos and games.

Two doors on either side of the container, nearly impossible to see if you didn't know they were there, would allow the team a quick way to exit regardless of the orientation of the container and there was an emergency hatch in the top of the container.

Jon held a meeting with the team with last minute instructions. He looked up and saw William enter the room and nodded. "Team, I think Mr. Braun has an announcement."

William walked to the front of the room. "You leave this afternoon for the port. The beef has been loaded. You will be on the ship by nine and on the ocean by eleven. People, the Lotus Project is a go."

The place erupted into applause. Cheers were sounded and there was a lot of slapping on the backs and high fives. Even the three Chinese joined in the merriment.

At seven the crew entered their home for many days and sealed in. The container was loaded on the ship at nine thirty. The tiny cameras mounted on each corner of the container showed the team what was happening on the outside. They could feel the rumble of the ship's engines as they observed the ship leaving the Townsville dock. They were on their way.

Shanghai US Consulate, CIA office

Susan Daley's cell phone buzzed. She picked it up and listened. She smiled as a voice told her the package she had ordered was on its way and should be there in five days.

Susan was concerned that Madam Wo may pick locations that would not be suitable for the delivery of the devices. If the devices leaked radiation many people would be killed. Every effort was being made to monitor her movements. Jai had assured Susan that he would have a list of potential targets shortly. The MSS had tapped her phone and would monitor every call.

Nu was in the MSS office when a call was made to Madam Wo's phone from North Korea. To their surprise the conversation was straight forward without any encryption. In a nut shell, she was told to have the targets selected in five days.

Nu informed Susan. He reported that it certainly looked like the North Koreans were moving their schedule up. There was no way to know if they had been successful with testing the device.

Susan did not want to call Jai. She knew he had been informed by his people with the same information. The extraction team was on its way and may be too late to retrieve Li Ming before the device is a success.

Onboard the Container Ship MSC Jade

The ocean was calm for a change. The ship made good headway. If the weather held, they would be a day ahead of schedule. The captain will earn a bonus and so would the crew.

Jon sat in the small common area of the container and observed the scenes from the cameras. Their container was stacked high on the deck. There was only one container on top of them. The GPS showed they were way ahead of schedule. They should be in Shanghai within twenty-four hours. He was thankful the ocean was calm. It was time for some shut eye. He went to his bunk and pulled the curtain. He had not been asleep for more than thirty minutes when an alarm went off.

Jon sailed out of his bunk and went to the common room where all the instruments were located. The environmental system alarm was flashing. There was some sort of malfunction in the air scrubbers. He called for Henry Bryant, the engineer in charge of the ecosystem, to come to join him. By now, the entire crew was awake and peeking out from their bunks.

Henry quickly examined the instruments. "The main scrubber is offline. The intake appears to be clogged with something. I am going to shut it down for now. We have four hours of good air before it becomes noticeable. I have to go outside to clear the intake."

Jon scratched his head. This was not good. "Do you have a theory as to what could be clogging the intake?"

"No, it could be almost anything. We didn't build a secondary intake because it was too hard to camouflage. The intake is about eight inches in diameter. Something large had to have entered and blocked the air flow. The only way is for me to go out and examine it."

Jon thought for a few minutes. The other crew members had gathered around. "Okay, the emergency hatch in the top cannot be used because there is a container sitting on top of us. The port side is blocked by another container. The starboard side is our only chance. That door will be dangerous because there is a forty foot drop to the deck. I don't think the bridge will be able to see us from that side. Henry, I can't order you to do this."

"Jon there is no problem. I can do this. I will need some assistance with the climbing."

One of the Chinese, In-Jung stepped forward. "I will assist you. I am an expert mountain climber." Jon nodded his okay.

"Henry you and In-Jung get your stuff together. Al, you and Tony manage the door. Keep your safety harnesses on and take no chances."

"Sir, yes sir", said Al and Tony together.

Within ten minutes the team was ready to open the door. The mechanism was simple. It was a long handle not unlike ones on the doors of a jetliner. Once the handle was rotated the door would push out and pivot on hidden hinges. The sound of air rushing filled the container as the seal was broken. The door silently opened.

Henry clipped his and In-Jung's safety harness to the eyebolt welded to the side of the container. In-Jung swung out and attached a quarter inch cable to the container. Henry attached the cable to his harness.

In-Jung cranked the pulley with the cable. Henry swung in free air forty feet above the deck. He waited until his eyes were even with the top. He couldn't see much because the top container was resting directly on their container. The intake was in the front where the refrigeration unit was mounted. The diesel engine running to refrigerate the meat was loud. That would mask any sounds he and In-Jung made. The air intake was on the side of the large bulge of the compressor unit.

In-Jung connected a rope to the hitch that connected their container to the one above. He swung out and around the compressor. Henry did the same. They both ended up side by side looking directly into the air intake.

Henry looked at In-Jung and they both laughed. Inside the intake were two huge seagulls. The pressure from the intake prevented them from leaving. "Okay, I'll get Gertrude and Hecliff," said Henry."

Henry reached in and grabbed one by the feet and pulled it to safety. The second one put up a fight, but Henry finally got his hand on the bird's legs and pulled it to safety. The two birds perched on the top container and squawked.

In Jung swung around the compressor and began the return climb back to the door. Henry was right behind. Henry felt something move in his utility belt. A large wrench became dislodged and fell to the deck below with an un-nerving loud clang. There was nothing to be done but get back inside before they were spotted by anyone investigating the noise.

Henry swung into the door way as soon as In-Jung cleared the opening. Al and Tony detached the cable and ropes. They pulled the door closed and moved the latch to seal the opening.

Henry went to the environmental controls and restarted the system. The alarm was silent. Each felt their ears pop as the pressure built. He turned and stared into all of the crew waiting to hear what the problem was. "In-Jung you tell them."

In-Jung laughed. "It appears two seagulls wanted some privacy and chose the intake to hook up. The suction at the intake was so great they were unable to get out. Henry extracted them and they are now sitting on top of the stack of containers." Everyone laughed except Jon.

"People this is the type of thing that can happen when there is a design flaw. A simple wire mesh would have prevented this from happening. Keep your eyes open for anything else. I know we didn't have much time to test everything, but now all we have is time. So let's get busy."

The team broke up and most returned to their bunks. Jon sat and reflected how close they had come to a disaster because fifty cents worth of wire mesh was left off the intake. He knew it was not his team's fault but they had to live with the consequences. He looked at the monitors and didn't see anyone investigating the dropped wrench. That was a bonus.

Chapter 29

Shanghai Port

The container ship, MSC Jade, received permission to dock. The process took little less than an hour. The port authority boarded the ship and inspected the manifest and gave the captain permission to unload.

Huge cranes began to attach to each of the containers. There were two cranes assigned to unload the ship.

Jon and the team watched the progress. They were to be loaded onto a truck that would take them to the local ship bound for North Korea. That process was hampered by the sheer number of containers unloaded and crowded with vehicles picking up containers. Finally an empty truck backed up and the crane deposited their container onto its bed and was secured with clamps. The trip to the next ship was short. It took only a few minutes for the truck to reach the outbound ship. The line of trucks unloading was short. Since the sanctions against North Korea had recently been increased, the exports to North Korea were down considerably. Within an hour, their container was placed on top of several others. It appeared there were only two containers high. Jon watched the monitors as the ship's crew made preparations for departure.

The ship's engines rumbled to life and the lines were cast off. They were on their way to North Korea. The seas were calm and the sky was clear with a bright moon reflecting off the water. The team began to check all of their gear and go over the strategic plan in detail.

"People, in forty eight hours we will be active. We have all drilled for many hours on each of our parts in the extraction. As you know, there is no way to plan for all possible events. It is imperative that we get in and get out without detection if possible." The team listened intensely

"Kow, your team will be the tip of our spear. You and your team will play the most important role in deception. You are there to arrest Li Ming and take her in for questioning. If there is any hesitation on the local guards, use the special weapon to disable them.

It is a harmless tranquilizer that will wear off in a few hours. They will not remember what happened. I'd rather have their cooperation if possible. We do not know what other security measures are inside the apartment building. With the rank of captain you should have the authority to arrest Dr. Wu without much resistance."

"Sir, all three of us speak fluent Korean and will use the normal bully tactic to gain access. You should hear it all over out com units. If there is an emergency I will rely on your team to neutralize any opposition while my team extracts Dr. Wu. We will come to the container as quickly as possible."

Jon shook Kow's hand. "Okay, that's the plan. We should be at the hotel loading dock at eleven PM. Terry will impersonate a hotel employee and will open the back of the container and pretend to unload the meat. The truck driver has been instructed to return the empty container at three AM. If all goes according to plan, we should be back on the outbound ship at eight AM. Let's all get some rest while we can."

A State owned hotel, North Korea

At two AM, the truck backed up to the unlit loading dock. Terry had used the emergency roof hatch to climb onto the top of the container as the driver maneuvered the truck into the narrow alley. Terry had on a white apron and hat. He would be in the shadows anyway, but there was no reason to be too obvious.

The truck stopped and the driver turned off the head lights. Terry hurried off the top of the container onto the loading dock and moved to the drivers' side of the truck and waved at him in the mirror. The driver nodded, dismounted and went to the service door entrance to the hotel. Terry confirmed the area was clear over his com. The container's side door that faced away from the hotel service door opened and five people dressed in North Korean army uniforms jumped down to the pavement. It was only a short distance to the apartment building.

Kow and his two team members walked in military style down the block to the front entrance of the apartment building.

There was only one guard at the front door. He looked very sleepy and jumped to attention and saluted when Kow approached. "I am here to arrest Li Ming Wu and take her in for questioning. Lead me to her room."

The guard hesitated for a moment but bowed and motioned for Kow and his two soldiers to follow. They arrived on Li Ming's floor where another guard was seated outside the apartment door. The guard from downstairs informed the hall guard they were there to arrest Dr. Wu and take her in for questioning.

The hall guard took his time getting up from his chair. He nodded and knocked on the apartment door. He stood aside for Kow to face the door.

Li Ming woke from the knocking at the door. She got up and went to the door without turning on the lights. She opened the door and was immediately pulled into the hall by Kow. He did not see any cameras in the hall but was sure there would be cameras in the apartment. Kow switched to Chinese. "You are under arrest and will come with me for questioning." Li Ming was stunned. She had no idea what this was about. The two local guards just stood like statues and watched as one of Kow's team put a plastic tie loosely around Li Ming's wrist.

Kow guided her to the elevator and told the guards that they were not to speak to anyone about this arrest until they returned in a few hours. Both guards nodded their understanding.

The elevator reached the main floor. Standing in the lobby was the man in the suit. He raised an eyebrow when he saw Dr. Wu in restraints and being escorted by an Army Captain. "What are you doing? I have not been told about this."

Kow walked up to the man in the suit. "I am here to take her for questioning. She will be returned in a few hours." Suit stood aside and allowed them to exit the building. So far it appeared the plan had worked. They reached the main road when shouting came from the front of the hotel.

"Halt, I want to see your papers", said the suit. Kow stopped and turned. The two guards were not with the suit. Kow carefully removed the special weapon and held it behind his leg. His two team mates spread out. The suit was running to catch up. He came up to Kow in a huff. The dart left the gun silently and the suit was caught by Kow before he toppled to the ground. Li Ming was wide eyed. Suit was placed behind a shallow wall. One of the men removed a plastic bottle from his coat and sprinkled something all over Suit's shirt and jacket. Li Ming could smell the strong aroma of whisky.

"Dr. Wu, we are here to rescue you. Please come with us and all will be explained." She nodded and followed the three men to the narrow alley behind the hotel. They helped her up the ladder into the side door. Jon was waiting. He was speaking in English to someone. Li Ming was confused. Suddenly several other men dressed in North Korean uniforms appeared and climbed into the container. The ladder was pulled into the container and the door sealed.

The Container

"Dr Wu, I am Jon Ferguson. We are the US Navy SEALs. Our mission has been to extract you from the North Koreans. We still have a few hurdles to cross but for now the hard part is done."

"Mr. Ferguson, thank you for coming to get me. I have a dear friend who is being held by the North Koreans. She has been forced to assist me in testing of the device. Is there any way to rescue her also?"

Jon had not been told of the assistant. He looked at his watch. "I'm sorry but there is no way now. The driver will be here any minute and we must get you to safety." The other team members were taking off their uniforms and packing away weapons.

"Dr. Wu, I am Shree Webster. I have some hot tea if you would like a cup." Li Ming looked at the American woman and nodded.

The tea was hot and good. Li Ming was still shaking from all that had happened. "I am sorry about your friend. With you gone, they will have to rely on her to complete the tasks. She will be treated well I am sure." Li Ming knew she was trying to make her comfortable. We have made a personal sleeping place for you. It's not home but it is comfortable and you can get some sleep. We are scheduled to leave shortly and will be placed on a ship returning with empty containers to Shanghai. It is about a two day voyage." Shree looked into Li Ming's eyes. She was sure there was pain, most likely from having to leave her friend.

***

The truck arrived at the terminal on time and the container was hoisted to the top of the stack. The camera monitors showed the deck crew closing up the hatches and getting ready to disembark. The sky had become overcast.

The ship moved away from the dock and eased down the river to the bay. The trip down the river and into the bay went without any incidents. The trip to the open sea would take most of the day.

The team was quiet and sat around playing cards and reading. Li Ming kept to herself and remained with her curtain closed. Shree asked if she was hungry but got a negative answer.

Jon was monitoring the systems. Since the meat had been supposedly unloaded the diesel engine running the generator and compressor had been turned off. There was enough insulation to keep the meat frozen or near frozen until they reached Shanghai. Their environmental system was being run from batteries, which would last a good week beyond their needs.

Chapter 30

Beijing

Jai Chun arrived at his home late in the afternoon. He felt he had been away for a month. His wife was busy getting ready to go to the play. He put on his Tux. "What is the play about?" asked Jai.

"A young couple fall in love but each of their families are opposed to a wedding."

"Sounds sort of like Romeo and Juliet", said Jai. He chuckled because Shakespeare was not taught in Chinese schools. He had five of his best operatives staked out at the play to watch every move of Madam Wo.

"There is a reception afterwards and we have been invited. Are you up to some social intermingling this evening", said his wife.

"I think that would be very good. I have been working so much that I have not had a chance to enjoy anyone's company for days."

His wife looked at him in her mirror. She could overlook small indiscretions. Most high ranking members of government had mistresses. She was not sure about her husband.

Madam Chun was not a looker, but was very aristocratic in appearance. She played that card at every opportunity. She knew most of her acquaintances were faux friendships because of her husband's high rank in the government.

Apartment building

Dauen awoke and went to the small kitchen to fix breakfast. She thought it was very unusual for Li Ming not to be up. She fixed a pot of tea and got out a bowl of cooked rice to go with scrambled eggs. There was a knock on the door.

Dauen opened the door to a guard. "Yes, may I help you?" she said. The guard backed away. She saw another guard sitting in a chair down the hall.

"Have you seen Pak?" She stared at the guard and realized he was asking about the man in the suit.

"No, not since last evening when he brought us home."

"Where is Dr. Wu? Has she been returned?" Dauen was now totally confused. *Returned from where? She's in her room, I think.*

"She is in her room getting ready for work." The guard looked around Dauen into the room. He was hesitant to go in. That was not his job. He nodded and backed away. Dauen closed the door and went to Li Ming's room. She was not there. Her bed had not been made and her daytime clothes were hanging on the hooks. She had disappeared and so did the man in the suit.

Dauen got dressed and opened the door. The guard sitting in the chair got up. "Are you ready to go?" he asked.

"Yes."

"I will take you down to the car." There was no mention of the man in the suit.

The ride to the lab was strange. It was just her and the driver. They arrived and she went to the lab as usual. The first thing she noticed was the appearance of several armed guards and three men in black suits.

She went to her work bench and put on her lab coat. She was about to open the cupboards and take out the instruments when Kwang walked up.

"Dauen, where is Li Ming?"

"I don't know. I was not aware she was missing until the guard came to my door and asked about one of my minders and Li Ming. I thought she was in her room getting ready. I went to the room and she was gone. Her bed was unmade and her daytime clothes were still on the hooks."

Kwang thought for a few seconds. "Come with me."

They entered the small conference room/office. Two of the men in suits were seated and the third stood in the back. As soon as they entered two of the armed guards took up positions outside the door. The man standing walked over and closed the door.

"You are in deep trouble. Your only assignment was to keep an eye on Li Ming and assist her here in the lab. She has disappeared and so has one of our men. Do you know anything about this situation?"

Dauen sat staring at the man. "I know nothing. I only learned of the disappearances when the guard at my apartment told me this morning."

"How is that possible? You live in the same apartment. Surely you would have seen something." His cell phone rang. He pulled it out of his pocket. "Yes!" He listened for a few seconds. His face was turning red and he was breathing heavily. He put his phone back into his pocket. He motioned for Dauen to return to her work area.

Kwang sat and looked puzzled at the man. "What has happened?"

"They found Pak this morning. He had been drinking and was unconscious in an alley near the apartment building. This doesn't make sense. Pak doesn't drink. I want every surveillance camera recording in the area looked at. Something is not right."

Container

Jon woke with a head ache. He took an Advil and got dressed. His first thought was their position. He checked the GPS. They were very close to the open sea. He thought they should have been in the open sea by now. He checked the camera monitors. The ship was moving toward the straits and would be through in an hour or so. He felt relieved that they would be in international waters in a few hours.

Shree Webster was up and had fixed a pot of coffee. Jon joined her and discussed the mission so far. They had a lot of ocean to cover yet and until they were in Chinese waters anything could happen. They had been told not to use any communication devices until in Chinese waters.

Most of the team was moving around taking turns in the two showers and getting dressed. While eating breakfast, they saw the ship finally move through the straits into the open sea. Jon was visually relieved. Shree was concerned that Li Ming was not eating. She went to her bunk and asked if she wanted breakfast. Li Ming said she would eat breakfast.

Li Ming sat at the table with four of the team members. She listened to them talk about the mission. They were young and excited. She finally joined into the conversations. She talked about living in Pasadena and her near death experience in Shanghai. They all listened with awe as she told about the arrival at the airport and the shooting during the taxi ride. Most of the team had never had an angry shot fired at them.

Jon was watching the monitors when he spotted a North Korean patrol boat heading directly for their ship. The container ship's engines began to slow and eventually stop. The patrol boat pulled alongside and two officers boarded. They went directly to the bridge. The ship was Chinese registry, so the North Koreans would tread lightly. After about thirty minutes the two officers looked around the deck at stacks of empty containers. Eventually they went back to the patrol boat and the engines started up again and they left the North Korean waters.

Shree speculated the North Korean's examined the manifest and because there were so many containers stacked so close together it would have been impossible to open them and examine the contents.

That evening Jon checked the GPS. They were seventy miles from the Chinese territorial waters. At the current estimated speed, they would be in Chinese waters in less than three hours.

North Korea lab

Dauen began setting up the test for the field generator. She had been working for about two hours when a commotion got her attention. She saw the woman Min Chang and her group enter the room. Kwang was in a heated conversation with her. He finally nodded and left. She came directly to Dauen.

"I will take over the test. Please set up the device to a full ion test."

Dauen stared at her. "But, it is not ready for a full Ion burst. It may damage the yoke coil."

"Just do it. I order you to begin the test." Dauen turned and began to hook up the power supply to the field generator. She and Li Ming had only tested with less than twenty percent ion flow. The system was unstable until Li Ming recalibrated the flow.

Dauen turn to the woman. "It is ready."

"Then begin. Go slow until you reach 100 percent."

Dauen began to turn up the ion flow. It reached fifty percent and an alarm went off. She immediately shut down the system.

Min Chang jumped as the alarm sounded. "Why did that happen?"

"The yoke coil is not aligned. Li Ming warned me that the coil must be carefully aligned step by step." She waited for a response from the woman. None came.

Dauen began to adjust the alignment. She brought the percentage up to sixty. The alarm did not go off. She hesitated but turned the dial to sixty five percent. The alarm went off.

"Fix that and I don't want to hear that alarm again." She stomped off to Kwang's office. Kwang had gone. There were three men in black suits sitting and taking.

"Who are you three?" she asked.

They looked at one another. One of the men stood and introduced himself. I am Seuk Dong-Suk, head of the GRB, North Korea's counter intelligence ministry. And who the hell are you?"

She stepped back. No one spoke to her this way. "I am Min Chang, head of the nuclear program for North Korea. I am in charge of this lab."

"Well, we shall see who is in charge of what. He stepped out of the room and motioned for two armed guards to step in. "These men are here to make sure you remain here until I confirm your allegations. Shoot her if she moves." Min Chang's eyes bulged and she stuttered that she would have his head.

Seuk Dong-Suk left the room and made a phone call. He smiled and returned to the room. "You are not in charge, you are simply an observer. Now that we have that clarified, you may return to your work area." She stared at him and pushed her way past the guards.

Dauen had watched the scene as did the others in her group. *It was amazing how she bullied everyone. How did she get anything done?*

"Dauen, please continue with the test."

Dauen nodded and recalibrated the Ion beam. She turned on the power supply again and slowly brought up the field. She got to eighty percent when she backed off the dial before the alarm went off. Once again she recalibrated the Ion flow. The alignment was almost complete. She wondered what they would do once the field was at one hundred percent.

The ion flow stood steady at one hundred percent. It appeared to be operating within the proper bounds. Min Chang leaned in and wrote down all of the settings. It had taken most of the afternoon to recalibrate and keep testing. It was time to go home. Min Chang moved to the side of the bench.

"Tomorrow we will test the Flux Chamber. Get a good night's sleep." With that she and her little group left the lab.

Dauen carefully dismantled the device and put all the test equipment back into the cupboards. She thought Li Ming would be very proud of her. She walked over to the guard and told him she was ready to go home. The guard looked into the conference room. Seuk Dong-Suk nodded okay. The guard escorted her to the car and rode with her back to the apartment building.

It was going to be lonely without Li Ming.

Chapter 31

Shanghai US Consulate, CIA office

Susan was concerned that no communications had come in from the extraction team. It had been nearly 4 days. She busied herself with a report to Langley.

Nu came into her office. "We just received communications from the team. They are about half a day out and all went well."

Susan was elated. "Thank you Nu, that's the best news I've had in days. Please inform Jai Chun and Nu, start making arrangements for keeping an eye on the book shop and the building they had used to keep the aunt. I have a feeling the North Koreans will be back." Nu smiled and went back to his cubical.

She picked up her phone and called the special apartment and spoke to Li Ming's aunt. They would continue to keep her safely there until Li Ming returned in a day or so. Then more plans would be made.

Beijing

Jai and his wife enjoyed the play. Surprisingly, the play was good. Jai had not spotted Madam Wo during the play.

The reception took place in a lavishly decorated room next to the theater. Jai spotted Madam Wo mingling among some top government officials.

A waiter stood nearby with a tray of drinks and small snacks. Jai got a drink for his wife. He abstained. He wandered away from his wife. She was busy speaking with some of the wives of the elite.

His phone vibrated in his pocket. He looked around and saw a door to a balcony. He swiftly walked out onto the balcony and answered his phone. It was Nu. He listened as Nu told him of the success of the team, especially about the role Kow and his group had achieved. Jai thanked Nu and expressed his desire to let Susan know of his appreciation for the update. He returned to the reception. No one seemed interested in him and he liked it that way.

North Korea High Command

The room held seven uniformed officers and one in civilian clothing. The general was pounding on the table. He was furious with the events that allowed Li Ming to escape. "How did this happen? Where did she go? She doesn't speak Korean. I want every meter of that city searched."

Seuk Dong-Suk sat with his eyes down. It was the Army's responsibility to provide security at the apartment building and the lab. He knew somehow he was going to be blamed for the disappearance. The general pointed at Seuk Dong-Suk. "Do your people have any clues as to how and where she has gone?"

"There is one piece of evidence sir. The army guards on duty say an army captain and two soldiers came and told them she was being taken for questioning and would be returned in a few hours. Strangely, one of our operatives appears to have been forced to drink whisky in an attempt to make it seem he was drunk. The man does not drink. So far he has no memory of the incident. My men are viewing all the surveillance recordings in the vicinity of the apartment. So far nothing has turned up. Some think she was extracted by the Chinese somehow. She left with her night clothes only. She did not take anything with her."

The general sat and stared at Seuk Dong-Suk. "I want you to find that girl immediately. I want to know every detail of how she escaped. Needless to say, your job hangs on the results." The general pushed his chair back and left the room with his body guards.

The other officers sat quietly. Seuk Dong-Suk got up and walked to the door. "If anyone knows anything about the captain and his two soldiers, call me." He knew if they did know he would be the last to know. He turned and left the room. *It's possible someone or group wants the project to fail. Maybe they sent this captain to remove their only hope of hiting the deadlines set by the chairman and make the plan fail.*

Cal Tech lab

Dr. March was elated at the progress. The new device was almost complete. They would be testing the ion flow that evening. The crews had been taking shifts and working twenty-four hours a day on the project. Li Ming's notes were impeccable. They reconstructed most of the critical items in record time. He knew they were missing something important but until they began testing he had no idea what it could be. His cell phone rang.

"Yes." He listened for a few moments. "That is wonderful news. When will she be back here?" He listened and frowned. "That long? Well I'm happy she's safe. I would like to talk to her soon. We are starting the first test tonight. So the sooner I can speak with her the faster we can get this thing working." He terminated the call with William Braun.

Shanghai US Consulate, CIA office

The extraction team and Li Ming were met with applause when they entered the conference room. Susan invited Jon Ferguson to give the group a summary of the extraction.

"Well people, it was not a piece of cake. The container worked fine but after the first week it would have been hard for any of us to pass a psych test." There was laughter around the room. It seemed to relax everyone. "The Chinese members did a suburb job in their roles. The North Koreans had no idea what was going on. The special weapon worked. We used it only once. I would give anything to know what happened when he came out of the coma it introduced. I'm sure there will be a lot of head scratching."

"Thank you Jon", said Susan. "With the extraction complete the project will be turned back over to Li Ming. She is with her aunt at the moment. She appears to have been well cared for and will be returned to California with you on a private jet. You should get a good night's sleep. The wheels are up at six AM. It's a long flight and you will need all the rest you can get. Everyone is dismissed."

The team got up and was escorted to the apartment floor of the building. Li Ming spent the night in her aunt's apartment. She had been told that she would be leaving first thing in the morning and to be ready to leave by six AM. She had to get her backpack. It contained her calculator. Susan said she would take care of getting the backpack. The backpack was still at the safe house. Susan wasn't keen on returning to the ill fated place. Too many of her friends had died there.

North Korea GRB office

Seuk Dong-Suk sat with his top agents in a small conference room. They had viewed what surveillance there was, which was not much. Nothing showed any unusual activity. Most of the images were at best only shadows. The GRB's best technicians processed any images that were suspect. They saw blurred images of several people walking down the road in front of the apartment but they did not seem in a hurry. No vehicles picked them up. It appeared they were going back to the hotel a block or so away. A man ran to catch up with them and appeared to be drunk. He seemed to collapse and helped by two of the others to sit down on a low wall.

They replayed that scene several times without any success of de-termining if the group was the bogus captain and his crew. It was not possible to make out any details. If it was the captain, how did they get away from the area? No vehicles came or left a six block area.

A truck left the hotel loading dock at three AM. They verified it was a normal shipment. The hotel people were not sure what was delivered but they remembered the driver coming in for a meal. He did not tell them what was in the container. After checking with the port, the truck returned with an empty container about three thirty and unloaded the empty container at a ship returning to Shanghai.

Seuk Dong-Suk was not satisfied with the surveillance footage. It was inconclusive. He believed she was still in the area. She had to be helped by friends that had access to uniforms and knew where she was being held. The nagging question was where did they go? They appeared and then disappeared at the hotel. The hotel people did not have any footage of the group entering the lobby. The stairs did not have cameras but they would have had to come through the lobby and would have been on the recordings.

Chinese Military Airport Shanghai

Jon and his team and Li Ming stepped down from the bus that had transported them to the airport. Li Ming slung her backpack over her shoulder. The G4 jet was waiting with the door open. They waited until the bus moved back to the gate before boarding the plane. They were in single file and started to climb the stairs of the plane. A man in a maintenance uniform stepped from behind a fuel truck and took several pictures of the small group boarding the plane. He immediately uploaded the pictures to a cloud account. He had no idea who these people were but only two appeared to be Chinese.

North Korea

Seuk Dong-Suk was awakened by the ringing of his cell phone. He looked at the caller ID. He sat up in bed. The attachments were several photos of a group of people getting on a large private jet. He carefully enlarged each frame. The second frame contained a woman dressed in fatigues but he recognized her as Li Ming Wu. The other frames showed clearly the people with her were European, possibly Americans. He knew who sent the message, and the location was the

Chinese Military Air Port in Shanghai. He jumped out of bed and hurriedly dressed.

He pressed a button to alert his driver to have the car ready. He punched in a number for his office. The phone was answered on the first ring. "Get all the group heads into the conference immediately. This is an emergency." The time on the phone showed 7:15 AM.

Chapter 32

North Korean lab

Dauen arrived at the lab as usual. There were only two guards. She opened the cupboards and removed all the test equipment. She removed the dust cover over the machine and looked up as Min Chang and only one of her staff came into the lab.

Min Chang walked directly to Dauen's work bench. "Prepare the device for the next test." Dauen bowed and began to hook up the gear.

Kwang came in and observed the little group at work. He went into his office. There was a message on his phone. He listened. There was an attachment. He brought up the attachment of a group of people boarding a plane. At first he thought who are these people? After enlarging the picture he saw someone that looked like Li Ming. He was shocked. She had escaped and was boarding a private jet. This may not be her but only someone that looks like her.

Kwang pulled open the drawer containing the satellite phone. He punched the recall button. A man answered. "This is Kwang, who are you?" There was silence.

"Sir, I am Fong,"

"Is the woman safe?"

"Yes sir. Would you like to speak to her?"

"Yes, put her on."

"Hello, is that you Li Ming?"

Kwang felt relieved. *She doesn't know Li Ming escaped.*

"No, but I was just checking that you are fine and safe."

"Thank you. May I speak to Li Ming?"

"Not at this time, she is working, maybe later. Put my man back on the phone.

"Yes sir what can I do for you?"

"Be prepared to move to a new location. I will call back with further instructions" He hung up.

Kwang looked out at Dauen working on the device. *With Li Ming missing, what will happen with the device?*

Dauen began to bring up the ion beam. At seventy-five percent she waited until the instruments were steady. The last twenty-five percent went smoothly. By lunch time the test was complete. "The beam is aligned. What do you want me to do next?"

Min Chang leaned over compared the setting with her notes from yesterday. "It looks ready to test the field generator. Proceed."

Dauen taped a few keys on the keyboard connected to the device. A hum began to be emitted from the device. Several small tools began to vibrate. The scope showed perfect sine waves. "It is working. The generator is producing a quantum field. The device is working."

Min Chang rubbed her eyes. "Okay, what is the next step?"

"We must bring up the transporter coil. That will take a few hours. It must be done in stages. Li Ming explained that the stages are necessary to develop an artificial worm hole. Each stage enlarges the worm hole. The last step is to give it coordinates."

"What sort of coordinates?" asked Min Chang.

"Li Ming said to use standard GPS coordinates but with a minimum of 5 decimal places. I don't know why."

Min Chang looked at the clock. "Go to lunch and when you come back we will test the transporter coil." Dauen bowed and left the lab for the lunch room.

Kwang saw Dauen coming toward the door. He quickly stepped out and motioned for her to come into his office. "Dauen, I want you to look at a picture and tell me who is in the picture." He opened the picture on his phone and handed the phone to Dauen.

Dauen carefully examined the picture. "I'm not sure, but the woman looks like Li Ming. What's she doing boarding plane?"

"Thank you Dauen, you may go on to lunch."

Dauen went directly to the small lunch room and took her lunch from the fridge. She was secretly jumping for joy. It was all she could do to keep from jumping up and down and shouting Li Ming has escaped.

She finished lunch and returned to the work bench. Min Chang had not returned. The device was still humming and all the instruments showed optimum performance. The quantum chamber was small. It was about a half meter square. She heard Min Chang returning.

"Begin bringing up the quantum fields. When you reach maximum, put these coordinates into the machine and place this in the chamber." She handed Dauen a plastic box about the size of a shoe box.

For the next three hours, Dauen concentrated on each phase and made copious notes. Min Chang came back and stood over shoulder. "Is it ready for the coordinates?"

"Not yet but in the next hour." Dauen paused and looked into Min Chang's eyes. She saw puzzlement and maybe fear.

"Okay, but make sure these precise coordinates are entered. The altitude is 165.89741 cm."

The next forty-five minutes went by and the final instrument indicated the quantum field existed. Dauen typed in the coordinates. She placed the box in the chamber. All that remained was to press the Send Button. "Madam, the device is ready to send."

"Press the button."

Dauen pressed the send button. Nothing seemed to happen. The scope showed a double sine wave. Then with a swish the box disappeared. Dauen was amazed. She really didn't think it would work.

Min Chang just stood mesmerized. She finally took out her cell phone and pressed a button. "Well is it there?" She listened to someone for a moment. "Open the box and tell me what's inside." She smiled and hung up. "It seems the transporter did work. The box went to its intended place.

Dauen was curious as to where the coordinates could be. "Where did the box go?"

"It went to a friend in HoHot, Mongolia. That's over a thousand miles away. Well don Dauen. Now how do we get it back?"

Dauen looked puzzled. "Get it back? I don't understand, Li Ming didn't mention that it could return items. I thought it only sent items. There is no button that says return."

Min Chang stood still for a moment. "You mean the device is a one-way device?"

"I don't know. Li Ming never explained the actual functions. Only that it was capable of sending items to precise coordinates."

Min Chang walked to the back of the lab and made another phone call. Dauen heard her ask for the general.

Min Chang closed her phone and came back to the bench. "Can you enlarge the chamber to take larger objects?"

"I'm not sure. We never discussed the possibility of how large the chamber could be. She mentioned something about not using the chamber. The object could be sent by using some other means."

"Have you searched her notes about the chamber or the other device?"

"No, I've be concentrating on the Power Supply and the field generator. The other functions were handled by Li Ming."

"I want you to read all of her notes and report back to me when you have a solution to enlarging the chamber or using some other means to send objects."

"How large should the chamber be?"

"It should be a minimum of four meters square and three meters long. Is weight a problem?"

"Li Ming told me that mass was not a problem because it isn't in the equation."

"Fine, take the laptop home and work tonight on finding out how to increase the size of the chamber or the alternative method she mentioned." She turned and left the lab.

Dauen had a mixture of elation and sadness. Elated because Li Ming had truly escaped and sadness because she was not here to help her with the device.

Camp Pendleton, California

Landing in Honolulu was only for refueling. No one got off the plane. The plane landed at Camp Pendleton, California and taxied to the terminal. The team was exhausted from the 16 hours of being cramped on the plane.

William Braun and two of his agents waited until all deplaned. He saw Dr. Wu walking and talking with Commander Webster. When they emerged into the main terminal building, William went over and explained to Li Ming they would be spending two days here to debrief.

Then they would drive to Pasadena. She was relieved they would not be driving anywhere today.

Commander Webster had made arrangements for Li Ming from the plane. "The bachelor officer's quarters are quite nice. I think you will like it," said Commander Webster.

William accompanied them to the BOQ. The sergeant sitting at the desk checked her in and gave her the keycard to her room. The room was through the hall door. She and William went down the hall. She opened the door. It was like a luxury hotel.

Li Ming asked if she could call and speak to her aunt. William made a few calls and handed the phone to Li Ming.

"Aunt, it is so good to hear your voice. Are you safe?"

"Li Ming I feel very safe here. They say that I may be able to return to my shop in a few days. They want to make sure nothing was disturbed."

"That's good aunt, I will call you every day. Bye for now." She handed the phone back to William. "Thank you. I think I will take a hot shower and sleep."

William nodded and left her apartment. Tomorrow was going to be intense.

Chapter 33

Shanghai US Consulate, CIA Office

Susan and Nu met in her office to discuss what to do about the possibility of the North Koreans checking on the aunt's capturers.

"I think they will send in someone to check on the original apartment where they took her. We should have a team there to intercept and take them in custody", said Nu.

"Yes I agree. We should have Jai's men do this. They need to interrogate whoever shows up. I'll make those arrangements." Susan called Jai and explained the theory.

"Jai agrees and will immediately make the arrangements to have several of his men occupy the apartment and be ready to arrest anyone that shows up."

Nu went back to his cubical. He made several calls and entered notes into the database. He knew the cooperation with the MSS was only temporary and he wanted documentation of all their joint ventures.

Beijing

Jai placed his cell phone back in his jacket pocket. Things were moving fast. Kow and his team had arrived back in Beijing and were being debriefed. He wished he could be in on the debriefing but the matter of where the nukes were to be placed took top priority.

Madam Wo was no longer in the room. She slipped out when Jai went to the balcony. He pressed the button on his sleeve. "Where is Madam Wo?" The answer came back instantly.

"Madam Wo is in the theatre next door. She went to the prop room and closed the door. When she came out she was reading something on her iPhone. She wrote down something on a pad and is on the way back to the reception."

"I want you to intercept her. Explain you are checking security and what is she doing in the prop room", said Jai.

"Yes sir. Should I take the note pad?"

"No, but if she has it in her hand ask to see it. Report to me what is written on the pad."

Theatre

Madam Wo got the GPS coordinates and the precise altitude of the prop room. The settings were to five decimal places. She wrote them on the small note pad.

She saw a man coming towards her. She thought she was alone. "Who are you?" she asked.

"I am with security. You set off an alarm in the prop room. What are you doing down here?"

"I came to check on the packing up of the props for our next show."

"I see." He could clearly see numbers written on the pad. He recognized them as GPS coordinates. He memorized them. "Thank you for your cooperation, you may go. Please be careful down here it is dark and dangerous." She nodded and left him standing outside the prop room.

As soon as she was gone, he opened his GPS app and stepped into the prop room. The coordinates 39.90426 N, 116.40742 E and the altitude of 16.36871 was displayed. They appeared to be the same as was written on her note pad. He opened the note app and copied the coordinates along with a note of where they were and sent them to Jai.

Jai felt his phone vibrate. He noted the message with the coordinates and where they were located. *So she is going to put a nuke in the prop room.* Jai closed his phone and looked for his wife. He had a plan forming. If he arrested Madam Wo now, she would not have a chance to find other locations to plant the nukes. He called his office and made arrangements to have Madam Wo picked up for questioning. This may be the time to show her the video and arrest her for espionage

Jai collected his wife and left the reception. He explained to her that he had urgent business and had to work late. She was not surprised. He didn't tell her about the imminent arrest of Madam Wo. She would hear about it from the news.

Jai dropped off his wife at his home. He drove to the underground garage at the MSS main office. The plan he had formulated would need help. The arrest of Madam Wo would be one thing, but making sure the prop room coordinates reached the lab in North Korea was another. He was in the elevator going up to his office when a message came in that they had intercepted a message being sent to North Korea from Madam Wo's phone. The message was the GPS coordinates for the prop room. He now had hard evidence she was a spy.

Jai went directly to his office. He phoned Susan's private cell phone. She answered immediately. "Susan, we have hard evidence of where the nuke will be placed. I will need your help with planning how to handle the situation. Can you and Nu meet with me?.I know it's late but this is very important."

"Yes of course. I will call Nu now and we should be in your conference room in thirty minutes." She hung up. *Well it seems things are coming to a head.*

Thirty minutes later Susan and Nu sat in the MSS conference room waiting for Jai. "What do you think he will want to do?" asked Nu.

"I don't know. But he mentioned that they intercepted a message sent to a phone at the lab in North Korea. He thinks she sent the coordinates for the first placement of the nuke."

The conference room door opened and Jai came in looking very frazzled.

"Thanks for coming out tonight. We are going to arrest Madam Wo in the next hour. That will mean she will not have an opportunity to select any more locations. We think this will disrupt their plans and may mean they will only be able to place one nuke device if in fact they have the capability."

"Jai, we agree to the arrest of Madam Wo. Dr. Wu is now at Cal Tech and has assured me, if we can confirm the device has actually been delivered to precise coordinates, then she will be able to dispose of the nuke somehow."

"I have already placed two men inside the prop room to monitor any such event. We feel with the current arrest of Madam Wo, they will try something in the next few days", said Jai.

"Okay, I will alert Dr. Wu and before I forget, your men have taken up residence at the original apartment where they took Li Ming's aunt. We feel they will send a team to verify she is still under captivity."

"Thank you for that alert. I was told a few minutes ago my men are in the apartment and ready if anyone should show up."

"Jai, this is going to be critical. Dr. Wu was adamant about the exact GPS coordinates of the nuke. I know this is going to be dangerous for your men, but we do not think the North Koreans will want to set off the device, but to only use it as a tool to force negotiations to go their way by threatening to set it off.

"I have thought about that too. It would make no sense to set it off. No one would know who placed it there and they would lose all advantages of blackmail. We now have to wait; the worst part. Thank you for all your assistance; I will not forget your cooperation." They left the conference room at the MSS office and returned to their own office.

Susan and Nu sat in silence for a couple of minutes. Then Susan's phone rang. Nu looked at the caller ID. It was from Jai. He pressed the answer button. "Hello", said Nu.

"Sorry for calling so soon, but my men in the apartment have just arrested three North Korean's trying to break into the apartment. They were armed to the teeth. No one was harmed and it appears these are not hired local thugs but real agents from the GRB. If we get any Intel that affects our plans, I will phone you immediately."

"Thanks Jai. I will also let you know of any situation that impinges on our plans. Bye for now." Nu ended the call. "Well that confirms our suspicions that they have had a change in authority.

North Korean lab

Dauen came into the lab and immediately saw several armed guards and min Chang standing at the device.

"Did you find out how to enlarge the camber?" asked min Chang.

"Yes, I found the setting to adjust the chamber, but the alternative method would be best. The chamber is limited, but the alternative is a field that is formed around an object. The only limitation is the power output from the power supply"

"So the question is, can this power supply create the field large enough to encapsulate an object two meters square and three meters in length?"

Dauen thought for several minutes on how to answer. "I read Li Ming's notes and understand the principle method but there were no notes on actually using the procedure. I'm not sure how to measure the field's size and how much power the power supply would have to output in order to reach the desired output."

"I want you to experiment on creating a field around an object. Test the power required to make a field the size of two meters square and three meters in length."

"I will need an object of that size to test. As soon as it is in place here, I can start the test."

"I will make arrangements to have an object brought here today." She turned and left the lab escorted by the armed guards.

Chapter 34

Pasadena

Li Ming, with her backpack over shoulder, came into the lab and was met with applause. All of the lab technicians had been told of her capture and escape from North Korea, but not the details.

Dr. March welcomed Li Ming and they went to her office. She put the backpack on a hook behind the door. "Dr. March, how far have you gotten with the construction of a new device?"

"We have completed the basic test of sending but the receiving system is incomplete. Do you have a procedure that you have not incorporated into the device to make it send and receive? I remember we did this several months ago with the object you marked for identity."

"Yes, I was afraid that if the device was stolen, it would be used for bad purposes. The test we did proved all systems worked. I removed the special code that makes the return from remote locations possible. I have it with me now." She opened the backpack and removed her calculator.

She motioned for him to follow her to the device bench. "This is not a calculator." She removed the battery cover plate and the four AA batteries. Below the battery compartment was a plug for a cable. She plugged in a patch cable from the computer running the device. She entered 625 on the calculator pad and pressed the square root key.

The send key lit up and a message on the screen displayed, enter remote coordinates. "She turned to Dr. March, it is now complete and ready to send and receive objects."

Dr. March smiled. "So the device the North Koreans stole will only send objects?"

"Yes sir. They would never be able to break the code for receiving objects. The original code is faux code and they would be trying to interface with the wrong module. I rewrote the code in Java to make it more difficult to detect. There is no one in North Korea that is working at the lab who can crack the code."

Her desk phone rang. She looked at Dr. March and answered the phone. "This is Li Ming."

She listened for a moment. "Yes you can send it to me at my email address, limingwu@caltech.edu and be sure to encrypt the message." She listened for a few more seconds. "I am very grateful for all you have done. Thanks Mr. Braun. Good bye." She replaced the phone and looked at Dr. March staring at her.

"That was William Braun. He would like for me to test receiving an object and sending it to another set of coordinates. I have not done this and it will require some additional software code. I can most likely complete the code by tomorrow."

"Well young lady, it seems you have your work cut out for yourself. I will leave and let you get to work." He left her office. The incoming message alert dinged. She saw a message from William Braun.

She downloaded and decrypted the message. It gave her two coordinates. They appeared to be far apart. The message said when she was ready for the test to phone him. After checking on the locations, she discovered the origin was Washington, D.C. and destination was Los Angeles. The message did not stipulate what the object was or how large.

She closed the door to her office and opened the hidden safe. The code book she used to insure no one could use her programs was one she invented herself. She didn't trust putting any of the encryption keys in her computer. The only code that was encrypted was the receiving code. It was in the stolen device but so well hidden no one would ever find it.

The remainder of the day was spent writing computer code. She would be ready to test the new code tomorrow. She missed Dauen assisting her. They had developed a bond. She only hoped she was safe.

Beijing MSS Office

Madam Wo sat stone faced in the small interrogation room. She was sure she was being watched through the one-way mirror. There were at least four armed men standing outside the door. She smiled.

They really had nothing on her. Only some GPS coordinates. There would be no way they could determine their use. She felt confident she would be home in an hour.

The door opened and a man and a woman came in and sat down. The man had an iPad. The woman opened a folder containing some papers.

"My name is Xai Ping Wang, this is my partner Leong Fu. We are here to ask you a few questions."

"You have no authority to ask me anything. This is most unfortunate for you. You seem to have a good career that is about to end. I have friends that will see to it that you and your friends will be properly handled."

"Madam Wo, we would like to show you a video. I'm sure you will recognize all the parties." Leong turned on the iPad and started the video of Madam Wo leaving the safe house. It lasted only twenty seconds.

"That proves nothing. I was visiting friends."

"Well, four of those friends are dead. The two with you are now in lockup and from what they have said; you are the one who pulled the trigger." Madam Wo appeared to be shocked. I did no such thing. I don't have a clue as to what you are talking about."

"We have your DNA taken at the scene. The men in the video are North Korean agents. You are their boss. In fact we found that you are actually Korean born of Chinese parents."

Wo jerked at that revelation A small bead of sweat appeared on her forehead.

Xai Ping got up and opened the door. "Take Madam Wo to lockup." Two of the armed guards came and placed plastic ties on her wrists and escorted her out of the room.

North Korea lab

Dauen worked hard all day trying to get the alterative system to create a field. The object they brought was a large piece of old machinery. The system would not complete the field. It appeared to work and then the field would collapse. The power supply appeared to be functioning normally. She had an idea. *What if I disconnected the chamber from the device and only generated the field without the chamber.*

She disconnected the chamber and pressed the keys to create the external field. A loud hum started. A curtain like blue light appeared around the old machine. She noted that the power supply was peaking but no alarms sounded. All she needed were a set of coordinates to send the machine to a destination.

Dauen powered down the machine and looked around for min Chang. She saw her across the lab talking with two lab technicians. Dauen did not want to interrupt their conversation. She decided to take a potty break. When she returned, min Chang was standing at the bench.

"Have you been successful in creating the field?"

"Yes, all I need are a set of destination coordinates to send the machine on its way."

Min Chang reached into her lab coat pocket and removed a note pad. She tore off a page and handed it to Dauen. "Send it to these coordinates.

Dauen powered up the device and within five minutes had a steady blue haze around the old machine. She entered the coordinates and pressed the send button. The hum increased and with a swish the machine disappeared.

Min Chang jumped as the machine disappeared. She walked over to where the machine had been sitting to make sure it was no optical illusion. Her cell phone began to ring.

"Yes. I see. Was anyone hurt?" She paused. "Was the machine damaged in anyway?" She paused to listen. "I will be there within the hour." She terminated the call.

"Dauen, I want you to document every step you took to create the field. Write down the settings of all the instruments before you leave today."

"Consider it done." She was elated that she had accomplished something on her own. She began to document all she had done except she omitted disconnecting the chamber.

North Korea High Command

General Park stood at the head of the conference table. There were six generals around the table.

"The device to deliver the nuclear devices has been tested and is complete. There is one problem. Our agent in China was arrested before she could complete her mission.

We did get one set of coordinates. They happen to be in the center of Beijing. Before we send the nuke to Beijing, we will send an actual nuclear device to a remote island for the final test. If all goes well, we will send the nuclear device to China in two days." He dismissed the group and remained in the room.

After all had left the room, he removed his cell phone and instructed someone to come into the conference room. Min Chang came in and sat down.

"Are you ready for the final test?"

"Yes sir. We have successfully transmitted a large machine the size of a nuclear device. All went as planned. On your orders we will move a nuclear device to the lab for testing. I will make sure the detonator is deactivated."

"Good, we have to move quickly. I want you ready to send the device to Beijing in two days." He turned and left the room.

Chapter 35

Cal Tech lab

Li Ming finished the coding and entered the final program into the computer controlling the device. She put the new code into the safe but was not certain it would work. She closed the door on the hidden safe and left her office.

She was still suffering from jet lag, but the worst was gone. She went home and ate her dinner and watched a little TV, but turned in at 9:00 PM.

The next morning, she was eating a bowl of Cheerios when her iPhone buzzed. She saw the ID was William Braun. "Good morning Mr. Braun."

"Dr. Wu, are you ready for a test yet?" *Wow, they are in a hurry.*

"No sir. I have only finished the reprogramming and have not tested the device."

"Okay, sorry for seeming to be pushy but we think the North Koreans are ready to send the nuclear device. We got a message from an asset in North Korea saying they successfully transmitted a large piece of machinery yesterday."

"I'm surprised. I didn't show Dauen how to create the external field. I guess she figured it out herself."

"Yes, well call me the instant you want to try the big test."

"I should be ready by the end of the day." She terminated the call. *Things are getting very tense. I hope my coding holds up.*

She went to her room and got two text books and placed them on the dining table. She opened her GPS app and recorded the exact GPS and precise altitude coordinates.

When Li Ming arrived there were only four people in the lab. Li Ming walked to the far corner where an empty bench stood. She punched up the GPS app and recorded the precise coordinates and altitude of the work bench.

She returned to her bench and began the task of starting up all the equipment. She entered the coordinates of her dining table with the two books and entered the coordinates of the bench at the back of the lab. She pressed the send key. She waited several seconds. Nothing happened. She powered down the wave generator and rebooted the computer. She waited until the message appeared to enter the coordinates. She repeated the entry and pressed the send button. She heard a popping sound and looked up at the bench in the back. There were two books sitting on the table.

With the first test a success she decided to test the reverse. She clicked on the icon that represented the new software program. She entered the coordinates of the work bench and the dining room table. The books had the blue haze around them and popped out of existence. Of course there was no one at her home to verify if the books arrived.

She clicked the icon again and entered the dining room table numbers and then the work bench numbers. She pressed the send key and looked up as the books materialized on the work bench. She was convinced the system worked. Now all that was needed was to call William Braun and try the big test.

"Hello this is William."

"Sir, I am ready for the test. I have the coordinates but you didn't tell me the size of the object or what it was."

"Yes, that was on purpose. This is what I call a blind test. Can you determine the size of the object from your machine?

"Sir, I'm not sure but it should make no difference to the machine. Does that make sense?"

"Yes. I was just curious. Will you tell me if the test is a success?"

"Yes I promise. Now how long before you begin the test?" asked Li Ming.

"I'm ready." William looked out of his office window to the four parking spots that had been roped off for the test.

Li Ming pressed the send button. "Okay whatever was in Washington is on its way."

"Holy crap, it worked. My new car is sitting outside in the parking lot."

"A new car was the test. You must be nuts to do this. It could have gone all wrong. A new car?"

"Well, it's not actually a new car. It was one that I was assigned six years ago. My car out here has been taken over by another agent. Thanks for the transport and it saved a boat load of money. "

"Let me know if any anomalies occurred to the car."

"You will be the first to know." He paused and thought about how he was going to broach the next subject. There was silence on the line.

"Li Ming, we are sure the North Koreans are going to plant a nuclear device in Beijing within the next two days. We know the coordinates of the destination. It is in the middle of Beijing. We have talked to the MSS and the CIA. They all concur that as soon as the device arrives at the coordinates you are to send it to a second set of coordinates. Do you see that as a problem?"

"No sir. Where is the second set of coordinates?"

"I'm not sure. Jai Chun has your cell phone number He will call you and tell you when the device arrives in Beijing and then give you the coordinates of the second destination."

"Okay, I'll be ready." She didn't like not knowing where the device was going to end up.

"When I see you again, I'll give you a ride in our magic car." He terminated the call. He had an idea of where the second set of coordinates was but he dared not speculate.

Beijing

Susan Daley stepped off the Air China flight from Shanghai. The new Beijing airport terminal was light years away from the old dilapidated terminal building that was pre Olympics. She saw Jai waving in the waiting room.

"Hello and welcome to Beijing", said Jai.

"Thanks. I'm sure glad this is about to be over."

"Yes, we will have to stop meeting like this." He smiled at the pun.

Susan laughed. "I heard from William and he says Dr. Wu's new device works fine. He is confident that within seconds of arrival in Beijing the nuke will be sent back to its origin or anyplace else we determine suitable." She watched for a reaction from Jai. None came.

"Susan, what I'm to tell you is top secret. The Chinese government has made the decision to send the nuke back to its origin. That is reported to be the North Korean's top lab for the development of nuclear devices. They will not know the device has been returned. It will not be in the lab but on the roof of the building. If they decide to set it off, then that's their problem."

Susan suspected that was going to be the case. "May I make a suggestion for the Chinese Government to consider?"

"Why yes please do. We have a great respect for your department."

"I suggest we take pictures of the device before it is returned. This will document where it came from. I'm sure they will have the North Korean flag and other propaganda slogans painted all over it. At the proper time, you can call a press conference and expose the plot and all of the players. I am sure this will piss off the North Koreans and they may even press the button. But instead of a mushroom cloud over Beijing, it will be over their nuclear lab."

Jai stood very still. "I will inform the government of your suggestion. I will drop you off at the Holiday Inn Crown Plaza."

Susan nodded and got in Jai's limo. The ride into the heart of Beijing from the airport was slow. The traffic was horrendous. She knew her suggestion was bold, but necessary if the rogue regime was to be stopped in its dangerous path of self destruction. "Jai, how much time do we have?"

"I am expecting the device to arrive at any moment. I have two men watching the room where the coordinates indicate. I will instruct them to take pictures of the device before we send it back. I was not convinced a woman, especially a young Chinese woman could invent and build such a device. But here we are. If not for your team in the very beginning, we may well never have known what was going on. Please accept my deepest thanks."

"Accepted with pride", said Susan.

Susan heard the buzz from Jai's phone. He reached into his coat pocket and pulled out the iPhone. "This is Jai." He bolted upright in his seat. "Take as many pictures as you can. I will call you back in a few minutes. Do not touch anything." He hung up. "Well it's here. The device is large and sitting in the middle of the prop room of the theatre."

He pressed a few buttons on his phone. "It is Jai; I need to speak to him now. It's an emergency." He never used the emergency card, so it got immediate results. "Sir, the device is here in Beijing. I suggest you and the ministers leave immediately." He waited for a response. "Yes sir. She is with me now. We have a plan but I need your approval." He explained Susan's suggestion. "Yes sir, consider it done."

He replaced his phone in his coat pocket. "The President likes your suggestion. He is calling your President as we speak. If all agree, he will phone me back with the official go ahead. "

The limo pulled into the drive of the Holiday Inn Crown Plaza. The driver opened the door for Jai and Susan to exit. They went directly to the bar, ordered fruit drinks and sat down. It was early afternoon and most of the seats were empty.

Susan picked up her glass. "Here's to a successful mission." Jai touched his glass to hers.

They sat and chatted for about ten minutes before Jai's phone rang. He opened the phone and answered. "Yes sir, I will confirm all when it is complete." He listened for a moment. "Sir, I am honored. Thank you Sir." Jai smiled at Susan. "It's a go. He was delighted at your plan. And yes he told your President who came up with the plan."

"Thank you and your President. What's next?"

"I must make a call to Pasadena." Susan raised an eyebrow.

"Dr. Wu, this is Jai Chun in Beijing. It is time. Can you call me back when you are ready?" He terminated the call after he heard her response. "She will be ready in forty five minutes. Care for another drink before the big bang, sorry just kidding."

Susan had to laugh even if it was the most nervous laugh in her career. They ordered another fruit drink and sat silent until his phone buzzed again.

Jai opened his wallet and took out a slip of folded paper. He answered the phone."Have you programmed in the origin coordinates?" He waited a few seconds. "Okay write these down, he said giving her the destination coordinates. Okay do it. Let me know when it is complete. About thirty seconds went by. Thank you, good bye." His phone immediately buzzed.

"Jai speaking." He looked over at Susan and smiled. "Thank you,

you may go home. Please send all the photos to the office before you leave. And thanks." He reached for his drink and took a long draw. Susan sat very still and silent.

"The men reported the device suddenly disappeared. They have loads of pictures. It appears to be a success." He raised his glass and touched it to Susan's. It was Susan's turn to receive calls. Her phone was ringing.

"This is Susan. Yes I just heard. I got it from the President of China." She chuckled. "I am not drunk, so good bye." She looked over at Jai and smiled. "That was my boss. He got a call from the President to promote me. I'm not sure to what. Do you have any openings?" They laughed.

Beijing Press Club

The press release with pictures was on live TV. The spokes person said the situation was grave. The Chinese Government was in session and considering what to do about their neighbor. War was an option being discussed.

A General of the Army explained that the deadly device had been neutralized and the public was safe, but didn't say how it was placed in China or how it was neutralized.

The Minister of Foreign Affairs spoke of upcoming talks with western counties and how this would not go well with North Korea.

Pyongyang, North Korea Office of the Chairman

The Chairman was furious after watching the Chinese news conference. He stomped around the large conference table. He wanted answers. "How did the Chinese know where the device was located? How did they neutralize the device?"

He pointed at two generals. "You have committed treason." He pointed at his private armed guards. "Arrest those two and shoot them in the court yard."

The two generals got up and were escorted to the court yard. Two shots rang out. Everyone else in the room froze as the Chairman began to stomp around again.

"Can we detonate the device from here?"

One of the generals stood. "Sir I have the remote device to activate the device, but the Chinese say they have deactivated it." He handed the remote to the Chairman. The Chairman looked at the device. He removed the protective cover over the red button. He pressed the button as he laughed with a high pitched voice.

Within thirty seconds all the phones began to ring. Each general answered and turned pale.

The Chairman scanned the look of horror on the general's faces. "What the..."

58473551R00119

Made in the USA
Columbia, SC
26 May 2019